"You've walked into something bigger than you ever figured."

A sudden burst of confidence boosted Janssen's ego. "One call and you're history, Colonel. My employer can get you busted down to buck private."

"You still don't get it," the Executioner said. "I don't give a damn. You can't touch me. I'm not in the system. Civilian or military." Bolan moved his hand so Janssen could see the Beretta. "And this is all the backup I need."

"So who are you working for?"

Even as the words left Janssen's mouth his skull blew apart, filling the air with a hazy mist. As Janssen fell the distant bang of the shot reached Bolan's ears. He was already dropping to the ground, Janssen's shuddering corpse following him down.

Looking back over his shoulder, Bolan checked out the hole in the armory wall. Big. The bullet had punched through with ease.

A powerful and deadly weapon in the hands of a skilled shooter.

And now Bolan was a target.

MACK BOLAN ®
The Executioner

The Executioner®
Don Pendleton's
SYSTEM CORRUPTION

A GOLD EAGLE BOOK FROM

W♦RLDWIDE®

TORONTO • NEW YORK • LONDON
AMSTERDAM • PARIS • SYDNEY • HAMBURG
STOCKHOLM • ATHENS • TOKYO • MILAN
MADRID • WARSAW • BUDAPEST • AUCKLAND

Recycling programs
for this product may
not exist in your area.

First edition January 2010

ISBN-13: 978-0-373-64374-5

Special thanks and acknowledgment to Mike Linaker for his
contribution to this work.

SYSTEM CORRUPTION

Printed in U.S.A.

The principal foundations of all states are good laws and good arms; and there cannot be good laws where there are not good arms.

—Niccolò Machiavelli
1469–1527
The Prince

I will use all of the weapons at my disposal against those who decide they are above the law. Justice will prevail.

—Mack Bolan

THE
MACK BOLAN

LEGEND

Nothing less than a war could have fashioned the destiny of the man called Mack Bolan. Bolan earned the Executioner title in the jungle hell of Vietnam.

But this soldier also wore another name—Sergeant Mercy. He was so tagged because of the compassion he showed to wounded comrades-in-arms and Vietnamese civilians.

Mack Bolan's second tour of duty ended prematurely when he was given emergency leave to return home and bury his family, victims of the Mob. Then he declared a one-man war against the Mafia.

He confronted the Families head-on from coast to coast, and soon a hope of victory began to appear. But Bolan had broken society's every rule. That same society started gunning for this elusive warrior—to no avail.

So Bolan was offered amnesty to work within the system against terrorism. This time, as an employee of Uncle Sam, Bolan became Colonel John Phoenix. With a command center at Stony Man Farm in Virginia, he and his new allies—Able Team and Phoenix Force—waged relentless war on a new adversary: the KGB.

But when his one true love, April Rose, died at the hands of the Soviet terror machine, Bolan severed all ties with Establishment authority.

Now, after a lengthy lone-wolf struggle and much soul-searching, the Executioner has agreed to enter an "arm's-length" alliance with his government once more, reserving the right to pursue personal missions in his Everlasting War.

Prologue

The background hum of electronics faded to silence as Frank Carella read through the columns of figures on the wide monitor screen. He reread sections, confirming in his mind what he had just seen, because as reality hit home he found it almost impossible to digest and accept what he was seeing. He leaned an elbow on the console desk and rested his head in his hand, aware that he was trembling—not with excitement, but from sheer disbelief. Studying the scrolling tables, the lines of test results and the conclusions reached, he spent the next ten minutes going over the data, until he finally admitted to himself that his initial reaction had been correct.

The Ordstrom Tactical Group, the company he worked for, had taken negative test results for high-impact armored steel plates used in combat vehicles being supplied to the United States military and had passed those false results into the production system. Carella saw, too, that the specifications had been signed off by one of the company's heads of quality control, and had been countersigned by Jacob Ordstrom, the CEO. The man not only owned OTG but also ran it like his personal fiefdom.

Carella had stumbled over the specifications by pure accident. He had been inputting fresh data into the company's massive mainframe computer, working on information drawn from other computers around the manufacturing complex. A momentary power spike had caused a blip, forcing the backup system to shunt Carella's current work into a safety file. It was standard operating procedure, a decision made by the online computer itself. Carella waited until he received the go-ahead to resume work, keying in the commands that would restore his data. When the file was restored to his monitor he saw a huge amount of extra data that had attached to the end of his string. Carella isolated his own data and saved it to a separate file, then returned to check out the mystery information.

The first thing he noticed was that he had been presented with data from a deletion cache. Someone had dumped a massive file, expecting it to be erased completely, but had neglected to key in the final code that would ensure no trace would be retained. Carella found himself intrigued by the large amount of data. His curiosity made him look further and that was where he found something that pinned him in his seat, staring at the document header. The file names rang a bell at the back of his mind. He tapped in more commands and began to scroll through the data. A sudden chill of unease enveloped him. He cross-referenced the data, moving back and forth, checking and rechecking. The more he dug the colder the chill became.

He brought up the current specs for the armor plating—the one being used in production. He applied a split screen, laying both sets of specifications side by side, and scrolled through the text. It only took him a dozen pages to confirm that the test failure spec was identical to the one being used to make the plating. Headings and dates had been altered, so the failed equations and tables were online as a successful development.

Carella froze, staring at the twin images on the large monitor. *What the hell was going on?*

It was deception on a huge scale. Someone had made a conscious decision to push through the below-standard specifications as the genuine article, and the inferior armor plating was being manufactured and fitted to combat vehicles.

Why would OTG let itself be compromised? Carella wondered.

He knew the company had been struggling to meet contract deadlines. They were in tough competition with rival companies within the armaments business. There had been serious complaints from stockholders who were dissatisfied with results and had put Jacob Ordstrom under pressure.

That knowledge pushed its way to the forefront of Carella's thoughts. He found he was having difficulty believing Ordstrom would allow himself to risk his integrity by doing such things. Yet he realized he couldn't conjure up any other logical explanation.

His next thoughts were tinged with anger. Anger at the thought of American soldiers being put at risk. Wasn't it enough that they were already at risk every day in the combat zones of Iraq and Afghanistan. This wasn't right. It couldn't be accepted.

He had to do something.

But what?

Carella slid open a drawer and took out a pair of flash drives. He slid the first into the USB port, then set the computer to make a copy of the files he had on-screen. He retained the split-screen function. It took the computer a few minutes to download all the data. Carella then made a second copy. He capped the drives and dropped them into his jacket pocket. He reconfigured the two data sets and logged back on to his original task, completing the operation. He saved the data to the appropriate file, logged out, gathered his paperwork and pushed back from the desk.

He made his way out of the computer vault, using his security card in the reader to open the steel door. Stepping into the brightly illuminated outer walkway Carella realized he was sweating uncomfortably as he made his down to the security gate. He recognized the guard on duty and nodded to him.

"Late shift, Mr. Carella?" the man asked.

"Seems they're becoming the norm, Lyall," Carella said with a forced smile.

Carella placed his hand flat on the palm reader, feeling the soft vibration as the machine scanned his fingerprints. A subdued buzz gave him the all clear and he stepped through into the main corridor.

"You feeling okay?" Lyall asked, noticing the sheen of sweat on Carella's flushed face.

Carella loosened his tie and opened the top button on his shirt. "Temperature's up a little. Feel a little feverish."

"You need to take something for that before it kicks in. Shot of whiskey and a good night's sleep."

Carella grinned, nodding. "Now that's good advice, Lyall. Just what I need."

Carella made his way through the Product Development Division, passing through two more checkpoints before he stepped outside. He made his way to the employee parking lot and into his car, where he sat for a moment, gripping the steering wheel and waiting for the tremors to pass. He passed a hand over his dry mouth. He really was ready for that shot of liquor right now.

He started the car and reversed out of his slot, swinging around and driving along the plant perimeter to the main gate, where he had yet another security check to endure. Clear of that he finally drove away from the sprawling site. OTG was like a small city, covering a massive acreage. It had, apart from development and the huge production facility, its own small hospital, restaurants and sports facilities. There was even a small bank on-site and a few stores. And of course the security division headed by Arnold Hoekken. The South African had a reputation as a hard man. He ran SecForce like his own private army. His dedication to the job came second only to his loyalty to Jacob Ordstrom.

Carella had heard the rumors about Hoekken. That he had left South Africa under a cloud after working for the state police. His work for Ordstrom was similar. Again, there were rumors about the way he zealously guarded his employer's privacy and had no time for anyone who went against company regulations.

That made Carella remember the flash drives nestled in his pocket. If his actions were discovered Hoekken would come after him like a heat-seeking missile.

Carella didn't allow himself to become complacent just because he was clear of the facility. He knew OTG's reach went far beyond the outer perimeter. What he had done was with the best intentions—to expose what he saw as a betrayal of the American military. He did not regret that action for one second, but he did accept he had probably placed himself in danger.

Carella picked up the road home, the drive easy because it was late and he had missed rush hour. The farther he got from OTG the stronger his unease became. He found he was checking his mirrors more than normal, expecting to see…

"Come on, Frank, what the hell do you expect to see? A big black four-by-four tailing you?"

He felt a wry smile curl his lips as he attempted to brush off the paranoia. He didn't succeed. He did become aware of his sweating palms. A sinking sensation in the pit of his stomach.

He forced himself to think rationally. He glanced at his watch. It was just over an hour since he had logged off the computer and left the facility. How would anyone know what he had discovered? That thought only raised his concerns. He had never thought about it before, but what if OTG security had a way of registering individuals using the mainframe computer?

"Frank, you have to use your code to log on," he reminded himself.

The mainframe held the company's most sensitive material, so there had to be a way they could monitor who

accessed it. It was common sense. OTG's complex manufacturing base covered a wide range of military product. So they
had to protect it.

"Idiot. You dumb-ass idiot." His shout of frustration was
contained inside the car, but Carella felt sure it could have
been heard across the highway.

With the realization he had probably left what amounted
to an identifying signature on the OTG computer records,
Carella fell into a deep mood swing. He was screwed. No
doubt about it. Once the record of his session was scanned and
the material he had been viewing exposed, he would really
be in trouble. The digital readout would more than likely
show that he had also downloaded the data onto removable
flash drives. The assumption would be that he had walked off-
site with those drives. Once that fact was exposed Carella
would become a hunted man.

He thought about turning around and returning to OTG.
Handing over the data and admitting what he had done. All
he had to do was come clean to Ordstrom. After all it had been
nothing more than a mistake. He hadn't gone looking for the
data. It had been revealed to him because of a genuine
computer glitch. A brief spike had put the information on his
monitor without Carella even having to look for it. Surely even
Ordstrom would see the innocence there.

"The hell he would," Carella said out loud. "Come on, Frank,
how do you talk away the fact you downloaded the damned information and walked off-site with it in your pocket?"

That was the thing. He had viewed the altered specifications and had then copied the data. Ordstrom wasn't going to
accept that had been a mistake, because it couldn't be.
Copying the files had been a deliberate act. Not a good thing.

And whatever else he had done, the fact remained that Frank
Carella had *read* those files. He knew what had been hidden.
Changing the specifications was a criminal act. There was no

getting away from that. OTG would be in deep trouble if the facts were released. And Jacob Ordstrom, being the head man, would catch the fallout. As big as he was, Ordstrom would have a hell of a job explaining away such a deliberate fraud.

So Frank Carella had dealt himself into a game that was about to have its stakes hit the roof. He needed to stay calm— to assess the situation and the possible repercussions. Because there were certainly going to be repercussions.

He spotted the lights of a diner ahead and, without thinking, pulled in to the parking lot. He switched off the motor and sat in the shadows, staring out of the windshield at the garish illuminations over the door of the diner. He looked at the lights but saw nothing after a while. When he moved he felt the flash drives in his pocket. For a moment he wanted to take them out and crush them underfoot. Destroy them. Get rid of the evidence.

The roar of a passing diesel rig snapped him out of his immobility. Carella climbed out of the car and crossed to the diner. He went inside and chose an empty booth. He ordered coffee. Through the dusty window he could see his own car, beyond it the highway. He was expecting that big, black 4x4 to show up. He would watch it cruise alongside his car before the occupants stepped out and headed for the diner…

"You want a top-up…oh, you haven't even drunk that yet."

Carella glanced up at the waitress, who was standing by his table with the steaming coffeepot in her hand. She was attractive, and the smile on her face was genuine.

"I'm okay," he said.

"Honey, you look like you got a load of trouble on your shoulders. Bad day at the office?"

Carella managed a grin.

"You could put it that way," he said. "But I got it figured now. Hey, how about a piece of pie to go with the coffee."

The woman nodded and left.

Perspective had returned. Carella knew what he was going

to do. True, he was in deep. OTG was not going to walk away and forget him. And he was not about to let them get away with their deception. If he had put himself on the spot, he was damned if he was going to give up without a fight.

1

The ending could have been marked down as inevitable but for the intervention of one man.

His name was Mack Bolan.

The Executioner.

It began for Bolan on a warm day at Arlington National Cemetery, watching with an old friend as a man buried his only son.

It began with the shadow of betrayal hanging over the proceedings.

With the taint of deceit and the cloak of a cover-up.

It began out of despair. With the plea of a grieving father turning to the only man he knew who could—*who would*—help.

Bolan, dressed soberly in black, stood a distance away from the main group, as Hal Brognola consoled his friend. That was the only incentive Bolan needed.

Colonel Dane Nelson was the reason for his attendance. It would have taken a miracle of denial to have kept Brognola away, and especially so on such a tragic occasion. Bolan was here for his friend. Dane Nelson was here because he was saying goodbye to his son. The military funeral was in respect for a young man who had served his country with distinction. Brognola, Bolan, Nelson and his son were all linked by an unbreakable bond that needed little verbal expression.

Nelson's request had reached Bolan via Brognola through a telephone call filtered through various links until it registered on the unlisted cell he carried. Mack Bolan had a small list of people he regarded as *friends* in an increasingly hostile world. His life cast him as a transient figure, moving in and out of the shadows, waging his unending war against those who regarded the world as their personal playground on which to act out their evil. Bolan never bemoaned his self-appointed status. He considered himself a fortunate individual, able to strike out against the injustice that plagued so many. They were in no position to fight back. The Executioner acted on their behalf. It cast him as a loner, having to stand aside from *normality,* so any connections he had with his small gathering of real friends were cherished.

Nelson's request had been, true to the man's nature, brief and succinct. He gave the date and location of the funeral, asked Brognola to attend, adding that he had something to discuss that wouldn't keep. Brognola, in his role as Director of the Justice Department's Sensitive Operations Group, had his suspicions about what his old friend wanted to discuss.

So Bolan was here, waiting in respectful silence as the crack of the honor guards' rifles brought a reminder that while he no longer wore the uniform of his country, he still affirmed his legacy toward its military. He had worn his own uniform with pride, had fulfilled his term and still felt the loss when he was aware of any American who died for the cause. He'd seen pictures of Nelson's son, Francis, over the years. Brognola told stories of the young man who was a carbon copy of his father. The last time had been just after Francis had donned the uniform. Nothing had been said but Bolan had seen the quiet pride in Brognola's eyes as he spoke of the young soldier heading out on his first deployment.

Now they were here, watching the boy being buried, and Bolan knew that the father would carry more than just grief in his heart.

Bolan stayed where he was until Brognola and Nelson

were alone at the graveside. Nelson's head bowed, his broad shoulders starting to sag a little. The Executioner walked across the green lawn and joined them, taking his own silent moment to offer his thoughts.

"Thanks for coming," Nelson said. "Francis would have liked it that you were here," he said to Brognola.

"Goodbye, Francis. I'll keep watch over you," Nelson said. He reached out to lay a hand on Brognola's shoulder. "We need to talk, Hal. I need your help." He looked at Bolan, who simply nodded.

As they walked the peaceful ground, surrounded by the silence that lay over America's fallen, Nelson pushed himself erect again. He was as tall as Bolan. Older. In full dress uniform, displaying the campaign ribbons and medals he had won over the years, Dane Nelson was an imposing figure. Still lean and fit, only the graying hair and the faint pattern of lines in his face betrayed his age. Bolan had noticed the lack of shine in his eyes. The death of his son had sucked out some of his pride.

"I need your help," Nelson repeated.

"Just ask, Colonel," Bolan said.

"No rank here. Just old friends." The voice faltered a little as he smiled sadly at Brognola. Then Nelson sharpened his tone. "They killed him. He was murdered, Hal. I know it." Nelson paused, checking Bolan's expression. "No questions?"

"I never doubted your word in the past. No reason to start now. What happened?" Brognola asked.

"Francis was investigating some kind of fraud that originated from the Ordstrom Tactical Group. You've heard of it?"

"Big corporation, heavily into military ordnance. Jacob Ordstrom is the president. Word is he has the ear of the main people in politics and the military," the big Fed replied.

"OTG manufactures everything from flak jackets up to armored vehicles. Ordstrom is a heavy hitter. His eye is fixed on the dollar signs in every contract he gains. Met him once, years ago, and I didn't like him then. Something about the man that made my skin crawl."

"You always were a good judge of character, Dane," Brognola said.

Nelson's brief smile had a bitter twist.

They moved across the carefully tended lawns. Nelson seemed lost in his own thoughts. Bolan and Brognola allowed him his silence until Nelson was ready to speak.

"A few weeks ago Francis was contacted by a friend. Cal Ryan. They had known each other for a number of years. Ryan is a respected journalist. An astute reporter. A smart man. After Francis spoke to Ryan he called me, said we needed to meet. When we did he told me Ryan had discovered anomalies within OTG design specifications. Test results had been doctored and ordnance put into production. Ryan made the first discoveries and began to look deeper. There were similar flaws in other items. When he checked them out he realized that OTG was falsifying test results and putting these specs into production. It appeared that by doing this OTG was saving millions on production and development costs, enabling them to complete contracts well ahead of time."

"Wasn't Ordstrom already making enough money?" Brognola asked.

"Ryan told Francis that OTG had gone through a lean patch. Ordstrom needed to keep his cash flow going, so the shortcuts were activated. Ryan made more discreet investigations and found the company was maintaining the deception even after their finances evened out."

"Ordstrom got a taste for it," Bolan said.

"Ryan said the man has a lot of palms to grease. Officials in the government's procurement departments. With all the military involvement in Iraq and Afghanistan the need for equipment is ongoing and vast."

"And the guys on the front line get issued with low-standard equipment," Bolan said.

Nelson nodded. "That's the bottom line. It's more, really. Ordstrom has connections with government, contractors. He's done some deals for the CIA. Worked with some suspect regimes. Ryan tapped in to sources that hinted at Ordstrom's covert dealing with illegal backdoor dealing."

"So how did Francis take it when he heard about the substandard equipment? I'd guess he was pretty upset," Brognola said.

"You knew his feelings for the military. He had a great relationship with the men he had commanded."

"Just like his father, if I recall."

"Francis wanted to blow the lid off the whole thing. He was ready to go rip Ordstrom's throat out. He took a great deal of convincing to take it carefully. Even Ryan made him promise to back off until he gathered enough material evidence."

"I see a big *but* coming."

"It all blew out later. Apparently Ryan had mentioned to Francis that he had discovered some army personnel who were involved. They were part of a test unit that had been signing off on the faulty equipment. No way they would have missed the substandard quality."

"Ryan must have been working overtime on this," Brognola said.

"I said he was smart, Hal. He was angry, too. At the way American lives were at risk because of what Ordstrom's company is doing. He was digging. Searching into everything he could. Gathering evidence."

"And Francis?"

"I believe that when he learned the names of the military personnel involved he couldn't stand back any longer. He was on leave from the army after his recent hitch in Iraq. As far as I knew he'd gone off on a vacation. I didn't find out until later that he went to this base and did some snooping on his own. He told me when he came back. Hal, he must have tipped his hand. Three days later he was dead. Shot in the back. The police told me he was the victim of an attempted carjacking gone wrong. They said he had strayed into a bad part of town. That was crap. Francis would have no reason to do a thing like that. He knew Washington like his own backyard. And he was a combat vet. Not a damn raw recruit." Nelson shook his head in disbelief at his own words.

"I pulled a favor with an old cop friend and he did some checking. The bullet they took out of Francis was military issue. Fifty caliber. Browning machine gun cartridge. The type they use in the M-107 sniper rifle. Since when do street gangs get their hands on that kind of specialist weapon?"

"You believe the people he'd been checking out got scared and arranged to have him stopped?" Brognola asked.

"It was all too convenient. Directly after Francis was killed I received a call from Ryan. He said he was sure OTG was on to him. He'd heard about Francis and blamed himself for getting him involved. I set him straight on that. Francis wouldn't have ignored what was going on. He went in knowing the risk. The same as going into combat. It was part of his job. Ryan told me he was going to pull back—gather all his evidence before he did anything final. His last words were that he would be at the funeral. I might not see him, but he would be there. I did spot him for an instant during the ceremony. Well away from the main group. I knew he'd come."

"Public opinion is pretty well divided over our involvement in the Middle East and Afghanistan," Brognola said. "It would make a big noise if it came out our soldiers were deliberately being sent into combat with faulty equipment."

"They already are, Hal. Francis must have pinned it down and paid the price. Maybe not in the field, but he was involved."

Nelson lowered his eyes for a moment. "Hal, I didn't know who else to speak to."

"Hey, you know I'll help. Leave this with me. You stay low. We need to talk, call me on this cell number." He recited the number. "Don't use your home phone or your office. Always find a pay phone," the big Fed warned him.

They reached Nelson's official car. A uniformed man sat behind the wheel.

"Chauffer driven now?" Brognola said.

"Goes with the desk at the Pentagon," Nelson replied. He held out a hand.

Brognola gripped it. "Dane, you know how I felt about Francis. There's no way this is going to be ignored."

"Thanks," he said and held out his hand to Bolan.

"Cooper, Colonel Nelson. Matt Cooper. I'll be in touch about that matter." Bolan raised his voice in case the driver was listening.

Nelson didn't miss a beat. He nodded. "Grateful for your help, Mr. Cooper."

The two men stood back and watched Nelson climb into the car. It eased away, following the curve of the road that led through the cemetery.

Still watching, Bolan saw a black SUV fall in behind Nelson's car. He nodded at Brognola then retraced his steps and returned to his own parked car, a rental he had picked up from the airport when he had arrived earlier. He headed out and kept Nelson's tail car in view. The dark SUV maintained its distance behind the colonel's vehicle.

Following the tail car, Bolan knew it was not a coincidence. The black SUV stayed behind Nelson's vehicle all the way across town. It had several opportunities to pass and drive on, but it held its position. Unobtrusive. Keeping at least two cars between it and Nelson. Bolan did the same, his curiosity aroused now.

Dane Nelson's story of the death of his son replayed in Bolan's mind. He felt for the man. Nelson's pride in the way

Francis had joined the military and served with distinction was evident. Bolan knew Nelson had done nothing to push Francis into a military career. He had allowed his son to make his own choice. A man chose the military because there was something inside him that needed fulfillment. The army life was not for everyone. For those who chose it the military offered a good life. Serving the nation was a calling. Francis Nelson had that calling. Once he put on the uniform of his country he became part of the family.

Brognola had told Bolan that Francis showed great promise, rising through the ranks in rapid time without favor from his father, who stood back quietly and watched his son's progress. Francis earned his promotions the hard way. He picked up his experience by volunteering for combat duty whenever it presented itself and earned his officer status after a prolonged stay in Afghanistan. He commanded his own squad. Won their respect through sheer dedication and a caring attitude for his men. When he was posted to Iraq he went with his own squad and served a number of hitches that saw them involved in some hard fighting.

It had, Bolan thought, been typical of Francis Nelson to step up and involve himself in the OTG affair. Once the young man had been made aware that OTG's deceptions were placing American soldiers in harm's way he would have been eager to help Cal Ryan expose the deceit.

Now Francis Nelson was dead. Shot down in his own country after surviving the hell of Iraq. That was injustice in Mack Bolan's eyes.

And if there was one thing the Executioner hated with a passion it was injustice.

2

Bolan kept a safe distance behind the car tailing Dane Nelson. Instinct warned him the occupants of the vehicle were not about to offer their belated condolences to the colonel. That time was already in the past.

Whoever they were, the colonel's shadows knew enough to simply keep him in their sights until they had cleared the city and were on the interstate. Nelson had a house that stood in lush forested Virginia hills, overlooking a placid lake, with the closest neighbor at least a quarter mile away. The approach to the house was along a quiet road well off the main highway. Bolan suspected that would most likely be the place for any move they might make. It was also entirely possible the men in the car were from one of the agencies, maybe even military, simply keeping an eye on Nelson. He considered that and tucked it away until the occupants of the tail car decided to show their true colors.

That came fast enough.

Nelson's car accelerated without warning, the driver arcing it around a bend and taking a side road that pushed into open country, with little more than open fields and acres of green trees on either side. Dust billowed up from the tires, misting the air as the car picked up the pace. The SUV put on a burst of speed, starting to swing out to run alongside Nelson's vehicle.

Bolan slipped his right hand under his jacket, easing his Beretta 93-R from the shoulder rig. He worked the selector lever by touch, setting the pistol on single shot. Then he swapped hands. Right on the wheel, his left gripping the auto pistol. Bolan powered down the driver's window, pushing his own foot down on the gas pedal, and felt the powerful engine respond smoothly. The car closed in on the SUV.

A figure leaned out of one of the SUV's left side windows, a squat submachine gun in his hands. The muzzle was aimed toward Nelson's car.

Too close, Bolan thought, and triggered his weapon, driving a shot through the SUV's rear window. His intention was to distract those in the vehicle. As the glass shattered, the exposed shooter threw a swift glance in Bolan's direction. Judging Bolan to be the bigger threat, he opened up with his weapon. Bolan felt the slugs whine off the rental car's roof. He didn't allow the shooter the chance to realign his weapon. Swinging his car to the right he gained a view of the shooter. Bolan flipped the selector to tri-burst mode and braced his elbow on the window frame and tracked in with the Beretta. He stroked the trigger and fired off half the magazine. With the rocking motion of the car and the erratic travel of the SUV, accurate fire was difficult. Bolan managed to place a couple of shots close enough to force the shooter to retreat back inside.

Nelson's driver used Bolan's intervention to step on the gas, taking the car away from the SUV. Ignoring any kind of safety precautions he throttled hard, the heavy car bouncing and swaying along the narrow track. The maneuver worked only for as long as it took for the SUV's driver to regain his own line of travel. As the SUV drew parallel with the colonel's car the shooter opened up, raking the vehicle at window level. The car veered, clipping the SUV's front bumper before angling away in an erratic swerve. It left the road and bounced its way across the uneven ground, the SUV following and moving to close in again.

Bolan slammed down hard on the gas pedal. He closed the

gap and cut across the front of the larger vehicle. Dust billowed as the SUV driver stood on his brakes, bringing the heavy vehicle to a skidding stop.

Bolan shoved open his door and stepped from the car, his Beretta already lining up as the SUV's back door opened, disgorging the shooter and his submachine gun. As the guy made to step around the open door Bolan hit him with a tri-burst to the chest. The shooter fell partway back inside the SUV. The moment he fired Bolan changed position, crouching and circling the SUV, catching the second shooter to emerge. They exchanged shots, the SUV man firing from behind his open door. Bolan had a clear field and he punched holes in the shooter's lower legs. The shooter sank to his knees, clinging to his auto pistol. Bolan triggered a final burst from the Beretta and the man went backward with a chest full of 9 mm slugs weighing him down.

Bolan ejected the magazine from the Beretta, snapping in a fresh one from his pocket. He turned swiftly back toward the SUV. He caught a glimpse of the driver fumbling with a weapon through the window, raised the Beretta and fired, shattering glass and hitting the man. He fell away from his driving position.

The moment he had delivered his shots Bolan climbed back into his own car and fell in behind Nelson's vehicle. The military car was slowing, lurching, as the driver obviously struggled to keep it under control. Bolan saw the car come to a sudden stop. He braked and climbed out, crossing to check it out. He yanked open the rear door and saw Nelson curled up on the seat. There was evident blood spatter. Up front the driver, the back of his uniform holed and bloody, was clawing at his door handle.

"Take it easy, soldier," Bolan said. "We'll get help."

"How's the colonel? How is he?" the driver asked.

"Alive," Nelson said, pushing himself up off the seat. He turned and saw Bolan's face bending over him. "You get them?"

"It needs finishing," Bolan said. "You able to deal with this first?"

Nelson, a hand clutching at his bloody shoulder, nodded.

Bolan helped him out of the car and led the colonel around to the driver's door. They got it open and eased the wounded driver onto the ground. The man was still losing blood and had lapsed into unconsciousness.

"Do it," Nelson said and saw Bolan turn and walk away.

As Bolan approached the SUV he saw the rear passenger door swing open, and a bloodied figure half tumbled from the vehicle. The shooter still had his hands clutched around the submachine gun. When he saw the Executioner he started to lift the weapon. Bolan hit him with a pair of 9 mm slugs in the chest. The force slammed the man against the side of the SUV, pinning him there until gravity took over and he toppled facedown in the dirt. Closing on the SUV, Bolan saw movement from the driver's seat. The man raised his head and looked at Bolan through the shattered window. He grabbed for the pistol holstered under his jacket, blood-sticky fingers slipping on the grips. He shouldered the door open, twisting around to face his enemy. A 9 mm slug took away his final thoughts, along with a portion of his skull, and spattered the steering wheel with bloody debris.

Bolan checked the SUV's interior. As expected, the vehicle was clean. He went through the pockets of the dead men. There was nothing to identify the men or the SUV. Their fingerprints might give some clue to their identities, but that was out of Bolan's hands.

He made his way back to Nelson's car. The colonel had located the first-aid box and was doing what he could to staunch the blood flow from his driver's wounds.

"How is he?" Bolan asked, crouching beside them.

"Couple in the back. Listen, Cooper. I called it in. Police and ambulance are on their way. You should get out of here. No point you getting involved."

"Colonel, I am involved. How's your shoulder?"

Nelson smiled. "I'm fine. Now haul ass, mister. I'll handle the flak on this one. You're better out there on your own. Last thing you need are the cops on your tail. Hal told me you were the right man for this."

"You have Hal's number. If you get anything from the cops that might help, pass it along."

Bolan refused to leave until he had fashioned a temporary pressure pad that he bound to Nelson's shoulder. He made the colonel sit with his back to the car.

"No moving around, Colonel."

"I won't. Now go. And stay loose, soldier."

Bolan stood. "You sure you can hold on until they get here?"

Nelson was pale, obviously in pain. "I have to. I buried my son today, Cooper. I owe him justice for what happened."

"We both do, sir, and he'll get it."

"Stay on this road about a mile. Take a right and it'll take you back to the main highway."

Bolan returned to his car and drove off. He saw Nelson's car shrink as he gained distance.

However he looked at the situation he was definitely involved. Fate had decreed Mack Bolan's participation and he would not shy away from his responsibilities.

3

Frank Carella recalled something a friend had said to him some weeks back. It was a passing remark during a social evening out with friends. One of those friends, Cal Ryan, was a feature writer for one of the Washington news groups. He'd mentioned to Carella that he was working on an article that was going to expose shady deals within the armaments industry. Ryan had joked about OTG being one of his targets. He hadn't said anything more, moving on to another of the group, leaving Carella with the casual remark.

By the time the evening was over and Carella was on his way home with his girlfriend, Ryan's words were lost in the slight alcoholic haze that had settled over Carella's thinking process. He had forgotten completely by the following morning, and back at work the next morning it was business as usual.

Until now.

In his apartment he fed the flash drives into his home computer and sat reviewing the data. A couple of hours passed. Realization hit home. Carella slumped back in his seat. He took his eyes from the monitor, the on-screen information a blur. He went to the kitchen and poured himself a mug of coffee. He stood in the doorway looking across the room at the monitor, trying to decide what to do.

And it was then he remembered what Ryan had said about looking into the armaments business. He hadn't seen or spoken to Ryan since that evening. It was not unheard of for the journalist to vanish into the woodwork when he was working an assignment. The man threw himself into his work, moving around as he dug for facts.

Carella picked up the phone and speed-dialed Ryan's home number. The phone rang no more than a couple of times before it was picked up.

"Cal? Frank Carella."

"Frank."

Carella immediately picked up on Ryan's monotone response. "Cal, you okay?"

"To be honest, no. I went to a funeral yesterday. Guess I'm still not over it."

"Hey, I'm sorry. Family?"

"You remember my friend Francis Nelson?

"Sure. In the military. Was in Iraq a while ago. He's dead?"

"Yeah."

"What happened, Cal? Was he overseas again?"

Ryan's short laugh had a bitter edge to it.

"He was home. Isn't that a bummer. The kid was helping me out on an assignment. Looking into irregularities at an army base in Texas. Camp Macklin. Sorry to tell you, Frank, but it was to do with your company."

"OTG?" Carella shook his head at the coincidence.

"Francis was found dead here in Washington shortly after his visit to Texas. A bullet in his back severed his spine. He was alone in his car. Police said the bullet clipped his main artery and he just bled out because the bullet had paralyzed him."

"Jesus, Cal, I'm sorry. He was a good kid. I remember him from the times we met. Lesley will be upset. She liked him."

There was a brief silence before Ryan spoke again.

"Why did you call me, Frank?"

"Would you believe it has to do with OTG? Something that will fit what you're looking into."

"Serious stuff?"

"High as it can go. Files on altered production specs for combat vehicles OTG builds under contract. I copied it all onto flash drives and walked out of OTG with it."

"I've been uncovering similar deals. Poor quality body armor for combat troops. Flak jackets. Below specification items. And I have a few names, too. Some government, some military."

"You think Francis was killed because he got too close?"

"Yes."

"His father must have taken it badly."

"He did. But he promised me further help if I needed it."

"This information I have, Cal. I came across it in a dump cache. Looked as if someone was supposed to have deleted it but they didn't complete the operation. These files should add to your evidence. What do you want to do?"

"Grab them with both hands, Frank. Listen, if OTG gets a sniff you've got this stuff they'll come after you. I know they killed Francis. That should tell you all you need to know. Jacob Ordstrom is a mean son of a bitch. I've learned enough about him to be wary. He has connections that go a long way up the ladder in Washington and the military. I need to get hold of that stuff and lose myself before OTG picks up on it."

"Will your paper print it? I mean, if Ordstrom has such clout, will it reach as far as your bosses?"

"Good question, buddy. Let me do a little thinking. I'll get back to you. Frank, I'm not trying to scare you but don't trust anyone from the cops on up. If Ordstrom realizes what you have he'll use any means to get it back. And that means he'll pull in everyone on his payroll. Just let me work on this. In the meantime, lay low. Don't let those files out of your hands. Stay by a phone."

"You've got my home and cell numbers?"

"Yeah."

"Don't take too long coming up with your master plan."

"I won't."

Carella completed the call. He stood with the phone in his hand, wondering whether to call his girlfriend. In the end he decided against it. Ryan's news about the way Francis Nelson had died rang warning bells. If Francis had been murdered to silence him, OTG would employ the same strategy if they discovered what he had walked off with. The very thought terrified him. He admitted that outright. Frank Carella was no hero. Just a man who had unwittingly been presented with information he could not, in all conscience, ignore. The accidental discovery of the hidden files on the OTG computer system had most likely made him a marked man.

4

Jacob Ordstrom's office covered enough floor space to house an average family. Ordstrom was ultrawealthy and liked to surround himself with the full set of trappings. A tall and classically handsome man in his mid-forties, his thick dark hair starting to streak with gray, Ordstrom considered himself to be above ordinary people, indispensible and existing on a higher plane. That he was disliked by most of the people around him was common knowledge to Ordstrom, but his wealth and position afforded him the ability to stand above the criticism. He walked in hallowed circles, being on first-name terms with leaders in the government and military. Ordstrom played on his popularity, used his imperial clout to gain favors and was never *behind* the door when it came to exploiting his influence.

OTG ranked high when it came to assessing companies who supplied the U.S. military. The products offered by OTG were sought after by the procurement arms of the military. And often there were inducements that went from hand to hand. Inducements went in both directions. Ordstrom had his own mouths to feed. He was, by nature, a highly competitive animal. He would, and did, deal with anyone, foreign or national, who came up with the finances. The word *scruples* did not exist in Ordstrom's world. He went after business opportunities with single-minded dedication. He had no equals when it came to the chase. Ordstrom had an innate capacity for seeing problems and dealing with them before they were fully formed.

Dealing with them. Crushing them. Whatever was necessary.

When Arnold Hoekken walked into his office, crossing to confront his employer, Ordstrom smelled potential trouble. He recognized the look in Hoekken's eyes. The South African security specialist was not known for his sense of humor, or his laid-back attitude. He was a consummate professional and he took his responsibilities seriously.

"Arnie," Ordstrom said—he was the only person Hoekken allowed to use the abbreviated name—as the six-foot-six blond-haired figure neared him. "Arnie, you're giving me that 'I'm pissed about something' look."

Hoekken towered over the desk, and glanced briefly beyond Ordstrom, taking in the wide view of the facility from the large picture window dominating that wall of the office.

"I need your permission to act immediately on a security breach. If we don't come down on this fast we are all going to be in serious trouble."

"Well, it must be serious if you're asking my permission. Haven't we established that as security head you work on your own initiative?"

"This goes beyond my purview."

The hard edge to Hoekken's voice alerted Ordstrom to the gravity of the matter. He pushed forward from the comfort of his soft leather executive chair.

"Christ, Arnie, now you *are* worrying me."

"Frank Carella was working at the hub. There was a minor spike in the power and the computer initiated a safe mode to grab his input. When Carella went back into his file it had imported the entire ASP22 document."

Ordstrom didn't react. He simply stared across the desk at his security head. Hoekken waited until his chief spoke.

"That's impossible. The file was deleted after Clarence adjusted the format."

"It *should* have been deleted, but it wasn't. Now Carella has seen it. The security cameras showed him working at the computer. The access log shows what he was looking at and also that he made copies. He was clear of the building before his intrusion was spotted. We need to find him before he gets religion and uses that information to bury us."

Ordstrom slammed his fist down on the desk. "The last thing we need is negative publicity with the oversight conference coming up in the next couple of weeks."

"Agreed," Hoekken said. "We need to clean this up now."

"Reading my mind again, Arnie?" Ordstrom grimaced as streams of thought crowded his mind. "That fucking computer. You know what we did wrong? We let the suppliers make that damned thing too smart. It should have completely erased all traces of ASP22. Instead it puts the file in a dark corner and sits on it. I'll sue that company for every penny it's got."

"We can do that later," Hoekken said, dismissing the notion and moving on. "Right now Carella has that file. He's out there running free. We have to corner that little shit and stamp him into the ground."

"You came in here asking for permission to go after Carella. Okay, you have it, Arnie. Find him. Do whatever it takes but make sure he doesn't get the chance to get righteous on us."

"Whatever it takes?"

Ordstrom nodded. "Wipe out his family if you have to. As long as it doesn't point the finger back at us. Use whoever you need. Hire whoever you need. Any problem there?"

"No. I have my contacts."

"Open checkbook on this, Arnie. Use the special fund. Christ, if this goes public it won't just be us going down."

Hoekken understood.

The suppression of ASP22 was crucial. Ordstrom knew the project encompassed both government and military individuals. Money, favors and promises of continuous cooperation with OTG had brought in more members of the illicit maneuvering. Any disturbance would quickly expand to bring down the entire house of cards. He did have protection from high levels, but any hint of scandal that might taint them would be frowned on.

Jacob Ordstrom, who had started his monolithic empire in a tin shed, meant to remain in his current position. There was too much to lose. He had used violence and double-dealing during his rise to power. It would lose him no sleep to have to use them again.

"Do you think Carella will turn the file in?" he asked his security man.

"No doubt there, sir. Carella is a decent man. That won't allow him to ignore what he's found. It's why he made those copies."

"Maybe he's going to blackmail us. Ask for money."

Hoekken shook his head. "Not Carella. Not his style."

"Fuck his style, Arnie. Make his new one *dead*. Get it done."

Before Hoekken had reached the door Ordstrom was reaching for his private phone. He had to make some calls. The sooner he alerted certain people, steps could be taken to keep the situation under wraps.

He heard the phone ringing, heard the soft sound as it was picked up. Ordstrom swiveled his chair around so he could stare out through the window.

"Morning, Clarence," he said. "We need to meet. Right away. Fine, I'll see you in twenty minutes."

IN HIS OWN OFFICE, down the hall from Ordstrom's, Arnold Hoekken was making calls of his own. He had contacts who were on retainer. Now was the time they could start to earn that money. Hoekken's calls were to disposable, unregistered cell phones presented to the contacts against the day their services would be required.

Like now.

He finished his calls and received one of his own. Ordstrom summoned him back to his office.

"COME ON IN, ARNIE," Ordstrom said.

Hoekken stepped inside and closed the door. He acknowledged the pudgy-faced man sitting in front of Ordstrom's desk.

"Clarence is the reason for the problem we have. He was supposed to delete ASP22. It was one of your assignments, Clarence, but you made a mess of it and now we are in trouble."

"Why?" Clarence Mitchelberg asked.

"Why?" Ordstrom smiled at the other's naiveté. "Because if the data falls into the wrong hands and we find ourselves being investigated they might uncover our other activities. Like the backdoor arms sales to unfriendly regimes. The financial deals we've handed out to foreign undesirables. Oh, let's not forget the money laundering operations we run through OTG's books for our foreign customers. All extremely lucrative and all of them fucking illegal. As well you know. Plus the manufacture of below-specification protective plating."

"It won't happen, Jacob," Mitchelberg said. "This can be smoothed over to protect you."

Ordstrom leaned forward, anger blazing in his eyes.

"You protect *me?"* he snapped, jabbing a finger at Mitchelberg. "It's because of your ineptitude we are in this mess. You were responsible for deleting those files. You made a fuck job of it. Instead of following through you let the computer finish off so you could go home early. You, Clarence, are an asshole. A fucking joke. Right, Arnie?"

Hoekken nodded. "He's right, Clarence."

It became very quiet in the room.

Mitchelberg sank back in his armchair, looking as if he wanted it to swallow him.

"I believe we've said all we need to. Arnie, would you arrange for Clarence's car to be brought to the front. I think he's ready to leave for the day. He seems to have something on his mind. Clarence, go home. Keep out of my sight until I send for you."

After Mitchelberg had left the office Ordstrom leaned back in his seat. "Early retirement?" he suggested.

Hoekken nodded. "Very early," he agreed.

The following day Clarence Mitchelberg's body was found at the side of the road, close to his home. As far as the police investigation could make out, Mitchelberg was the victim of a hit-and-run. There were no witnesses.

5

"Colonel Stone, Special Agent, Army CID," Bolan said, showing the holder carrying the badge and his ID card. "Here on official business, Corporal Huston. This is an unannounced inspection."

The sentry at the gate of the Camp Macklin Texas military base checked the ID and the man sitting at the wheel of the gleaming black Crown Victoria. The ID stated that Brandon Stone was indeed a colonel in the Army Criminal Investigation Division. Carl Huston knew enough about the investigators from CID not to screw around with the man.... On the other hand he also knew they expected professional conduct from anyone who came into contact with them. Huston threw a sharp, by-the-book salute. One look at the grim-faced colonel and Huston knew the guy was for real.

"So you are not expected, sir?" he asked.

Mack Bolan took the ID back, giving the sentry a cold stare.

"If I let everyone know I was coming I'd never catch them in the act, would I, Corporal?"

"No, sir."

"That's why it is designated as an unannounced inspection. You go about your duties, Huston. I'll inform those who need to know that I'm here." Bolan nodded in the direction of the barrier and waited until Huston pressed the button to raise it. "Carry on, Corporal."

Huston watched the car drive onto the base. He lowered the barrier as he stepped back inside the hut. His hand reached for the phone, then drew back. If he let the base commander know CID was on the way, Stone would know. Colonel Bosley was a good CO, but he was no gung-ho hard man. Bosley liked things to run quiet and smooth. And he was no actor. The moment Stone walked into his office Bosley would give himself away. Bosley might give Huston a dressing down later. That was preferable to upsetting a hard-ass like Stone, and definitely preferable to getting on the CID's list as not being trustworthy.

BOLAN FOLLOWED THE marked signs that showed the way to Camp Macklin's HQ building. It had been some time since he had set foot on a military base. It had been a longer time since he had been in the service himself, but the feeling was still there—the sense of belonging to the extended family that permeated the base. It never left a man once he had worn the uniform.

Bolan studied the buildings, the neat layout of the place. In the distance he picked up the sound of men being drilled, the instructors' commands carrying across the base. Time moved on but the very essence of military life remained constant. When he parked alongside the other vehicles outside the HQ building and stepped out, Bolan stood and let the ambience wash over him. Then he turned and strode toward the building, affecting the ingrained stance of a military man, despite being dressed in a civilian suit, white shirt and dark tie, the day-to-day uniform of a CID agent.

Walking into the outer office Bolan caught the attention of the army clerk behind one of the desks. The office was empty save for the young soldier.

"Colonel Stone, CID, to see Colonel Bosley," Bolan snapped. He held out his ID. "Is he in?"

"Yes, sir, Colonel Stone."

"Show me the way, Curtis," Bolan said, reading the name tag on the man's uniform.

Private Curtis sprang to his feet, saluting, then moved with surprising speed. He led Bolan along the passage to the door at the end. He knocked and entered on command.

"Colonel will see you now, sir," Curtis said when he ducked out again. He held the door for Bolan to enter, then closed it quietly as he stepped back outside.

Colonel Bosley was around fifty and starting to show the effects of his easy command—a noticeable bulge at the waist beneath his crisp uniform shirt. His thinning hair was gray. He pushed to his feet as Bolan crossed to face him over the desk.

"Take a seat."

When they were seated Bolan passed his ID across to the colonel. Bosley examined it and passed it back.

"I suppose surprise visits are to be expected," Bosley said, his tone easy. "What can I do for you, Stone?"

"I need to talk to certain of your people here. Because of circumstances surrounding an ongoing investigation I can't give you much detail. Let's just say this is a major investigation with possible far-reaching implications."

"Not trying to be flippant, Colonel, but you make it sound serious."

"It is. Command is trying to keep it low-key until we gather more evidence. They don't want word getting out that might alert suspects. That's why I need your cooperation, Colonel."

"Of course. Anything I can do?"

"Just let me conduct my investigation unhindered. I'll try and keep it as quiet as possible and try not to upset anyone I don't need to."

"If anyone refuses to help refer them to me, Colonel."

"Thank you, Colonel Bosley. I'll make sure Command gets to hear of your cooperation."

Bolan rose and shook Bosley's hand.

"Just one other thing, Colonel," Bolan said, opening his jacket. "I am armed." Bolan wore his standard issue Beretta M9 in military shoulder rig. He would have preferred his 93-R, but this masquerade demanded he follow protocol and CID colonels would not walk around displaying a specialized Beretta.

"As you said, Colonel, a serious investigation," Bosley said.

"Would you direct me to the test area," Bolan said.

Bosley found it hard to conceal his surprise at the request. Whatever he might have been wondering about the surprise visit from CID, he had been hoping the base test and assessment section would not be on any list. He kept questions to himself, pushing to his feet and crossing his office to the large wall map showing the layout of the base.

"This is where we are." He indicated the location as Bolan joined him. "The test area is here, three miles north. You need to take this route. Once you clear the main base it's the only road. Just stay on it and you'll reach the area."

"Any testing taking place at the moment?"

Bosley shook his head. "Nothing scheduled for a couple of days, so the area will be quiet. Just the permanent staff on duty." Bosley turned to his desk and checked a document. "There's a civilian representative from OTG, one of our main contractors, on-site."

"Thank you, Colonel Bosley."

"They're pretty tight on security out there," Bosley said. "You have any problems just get someone to pick up the phone and call me. I'll clear any queries. In the meantime tell Private Curtis to issue you with a clearance pass."

ON THE WAY OUT the Executioner stopped at the private's desk and was handed a laminated tag that he clipped to his jacket. Back in his car he cranked up the air-conditioning and let cool air wash over him. He slipped on the aviator shades he'd left inside the car and drove away from the HQ building, follow-

ing Bosley's directions. He picked up the route and drove
through the base until he found himself on the northbound
road. The base fell behind him. In his rearview mirror all he
could see was the pale cloud of dust rising in his wake.

Bolan stopped once, taking out the Beretta and checking
the magazine. He slid it back in, worked the slide and fed the
first 9 mm into place. He made sure the safety was off before
he reholstered the weapon. It was a natural reaction to a potentially difficult situation. Mack Bolan had survived for this
long by treating every unknown quantity as potentially life
threatening. Any venture into new territory carried its own
particular possibility of threat. If someone thrust a cocked gun
in his face it was far too late to ask for time to prepare his own
weapon. It wasn't from a feeling of paranoia, more a simple
survival reflex, and it had served the Executioner well. And,
he decided wryly, he was too old to change his ways.

Around him the terrain had taken on a wilderness aspect—
mostly flatland, with a few shallow depressions and humped
ridges. Much farther to the north the hazy rise of low hills
could be seen. There was scarce vegetation, dusty scrub, a
scattering of skinny trees. He saw slight movement caused by
a hot breeze, heard the scratchy hiss of gritty dust striking the
sides of the car. He passed a few signs warning he would soon
be entering a test area.

A long slope ahead showed Bolan the beginning of the area
proper. There were a number of long huts. Workshops. An
enclosed area that would likely hold munitions. He saw an open
communications bunker, with a radar dish and aerials. Vehicles
were in evidence. All military except for one civilian car.

The road ended at a checkpoint. Bolan watched as an
armed sentry stepped out and planted himself in front of the
car. Bolan braked and powered down his window, waiting.
The sentry strode around and stared at Bolan, who had his ID
out and in full view.

"Out of the car," the sentry snapped.

"Read the ID, soldier, then address me by my rank."

The sentry leaned forward and scanned the ID. When he realized he was in the presence of a colonel *and* a CID agent, he pulled back.

"Sorry, Colonel, sir. Just following procedure, sir."

Bolan stepped out of the car, taking off his aviator shades. He checked out the sentry's name tag.

"No problem with that, Conner." Bolan tapped the security tag on his jacket. "If you need verification call Colonel Bosley. I was just with him."

Conner shook his head. "Your pass gives you clearance, Colonel."

"Who's in command here, Conner?" Bolan asked.

"I am...sir," a voice said.

Bolan glanced around and got his first look at Master Sergeant Thomas K. Randisi. The man was as tall as Bolan. Broad, erect. Every inch the professional soldier. Even in the dry, dusty heat his uniform looked as if it had just been pressed. His gleaming boots defied dust to settle on them.

As Bolan confronted him, Randisi slid off his dark glasses. His gray eyes held a gleam of defiance. He was deeply tanned, his high-boned features weathered. Down his left cheek was a slight pattern of pale scars. The man was military from his boot tips to the top of his close-shaved head, and he was showing Bolan that he was not in the least intimidated by a colonel, even one from CID.

"Master Sergeant Randisi," Bolan said. "Just the man I want to talk to." He flashed his ID at Randisi. "Just so we get off on the right foot."

"What can I do for you, Colonel?"

"A few questions first." Bolan glanced at the sentry. "Dismissed, Conner."

Bolan did not miss the questioning glance Conner shot in

Randisi's direction. There was no flicker of unease in the master sergeant's eyes. He simply nodded curtly, and Conner returned to his post.

"Questions, sir?" Randisi asked. "Why would CID be interested in us?"

"I ask the questions, Randisi. That's how it works." Bolan kept his tone light but with enough authority to keep Randisi wondering. "Let's go and check out your civilian presence here."

"Mr. Janssen has full clearance," Randisi said as they strode in the direction of the main building. "He's a regular visitor. Monitors our assessment and testing of OTG products."

"That's wise considering the current situation, Master Sergeant," Bolan said out of the blue, leaving Randisi staring at him, unsure what was being suggested.

The interior of the long hut was fitted out as a control center and office. A balding, lanky man in civilian dress was turning from a water cooler as Bolan and Randisi entered. The man looked past Bolan to Randisi.

"Stefan Janssen, isn't it?" Bolan said briskly. "I seem to be meeting all the names on my list at the same time."

"Colonel Stone is from Army CID," Randisi said, jumping in quickly.

"Criminal investigation," Bolan said. "We handle policing for the army."

The paper cup in Janssen's hand jerked, spilling water that splashed his shirt front.

"Nervous, Mr. Janssen?" Bolan asked.

Janssen's flushed face gave away his feelings. He brushed at the spilled water. "No. Should I be?"

Bolan gave him a tight smile. "You tell me, Mr. Janssen. I just got here."

Janssen's pitiful glance at Bolan might have been an attempt to draw sympathy. Bolan wasn't in a forgiving mood. He held Janssen's uneasy stare for long seconds.

"As I explained, Colonel," Randisi said from behind Bolan, "Mr. Janssen is here courtesy of the army. He's a guest."

Janssen seemed to draw strength from Randisi's endorsement. He swallowed the contents of the paper cup.

"You should know, Colonel Stone, that my company, OTG, is held in great esteem by the Pentagon. We have supplied ordnance for a long time. My employer, Jacob Ordstrom, has highly placed contacts within…"

"Two things, Janssen," Bolan said, dropping the niceties. "CID is not interested in who your employer is in bed with. I'm here to investigate serious irregularities regarding equipment supply and supposed testing of said equipment. Don't try and impress me with name dropping, sir. I am *not* impressed. I am not intimidated. And it appears that when you mentioned Ordstrom I feel sure I've seen his name on a list, as well. It would appear, Mr. Janssen, I'm having a better day than I anticipated."

Bolan sensed movement behind him. He stepped to one side, turning, and saw that Randisi had stepped to one side of the hut, close to a desk where an unholstered sidearm lay in clear sight. "Just what is it CID is interested in, Colonel?" he asked.

"I was hoping you could provide me with some answers there, Randisi. The information we have makes tenuous links between the death of a young army officer and a missing employee from OTG."

"I don't understand, Colonel," Randisi said calmly. "You said an army officer?"

"Lieutenant Francis Nelson. My information is that he visited this camp a short time ago. He was killed on his return to Washington.

"Killed?"

"To be specific, he was murdered. I tracked down the police forensic report and it appears he was hit by a .50-caliber bullet. The type they use in the M-107 military sniper rifle. Like that one in the rack over there."

Bolan crossed to inspect the rifle. He studied it closely, listening as Randisi walked across to stand behind him.

"Your specialty, Master Sergeant, by the sharpshooter insignia you're wearing."

"That's correct, Colonel. A sharpshooter's badge. You take a walk around camp, you'll see a few more. I'm not the only one who has that distinction."

Bolan turned around to face Randisi. He held the master sergeant's unflinching stare.

"I have one myself, Randisi. And I keep my hand in. You never know when it might come in useful."

"That you don't, sir."

Bolan smiled briefly, then stepped around Randisi and joined the nervous Janssen. The OTG man was standing at the open door, and Bolan had the feeling the man was close to making a run for it. Wet patches showed under Janssen's armpits and his face gleamed.

"Gets really hot in this part of the country, Mr. Janssen. You feeling the heat right now?" the Executioner asked.

"I'm fine."

"The OTG man I mentioned earlier was named Frank Carella. Do you know him, Mr. Janssen?"

"You realize how large OTG is, Colonel? There are people there I wouldn't know if they walked in here right now."

"I take that as a no?"

"You can…"

"Excuse me, Colonel," Randisi said quickly. "You will have to make allowances for Mr. Janssen. He hasn't taken to our climate too well."

Bolan held his stare on Janssen. He wanted the man to be uncomfortable. He sensed a weakness in his makeup. He felt Janssen might talk if he was pushed hard enough. It was time to let the man consider his position. Walking away would leave Janssen wondering what was going to happen next.

"Fine, Randisi. That will do for today. But make yourselves available tomorrow. We *will* need to talk again."

6

The Sunbird Motor Court sat alongside the highway, next to a long diner and adjacent to a gas station, ten miles from the camp. An oasis in the scrubland. To the side of the gas station was a flattened patch of land that served as the parking lot for the big rigs and cars that traversed the highway. It was a dusty setup, not helped by the semipermanent, arid breeze that was as much part of the landscape as the brittle grass and spiky scrub.

Bolan's cabin overlooked the highway and the terrain beyond. It would never win any prizes for the most pleasing aspect from a motel window, but that wasn't Bolan's reason for the occasional glance through the dusty glass.

He had a feeling his visit to Camp Macklin had generated enough unrest to warrant a response. Bolan couldn't prove out his feeling. It was just a natural response to the situation. Standing at the cabin's window, cup of coffee in his hand, he turned to look at the Beretta 93-R and the Desert Eagle lying side by side on the bed.

Was he going to need them?

Would his enemies show up here, rather than wait for their chance when he drove on? Any decision they made depended on how desperate they were to guarantee his silence. Going on their previous form with the attack on Dane Nelson, subtlety was not on the agenda.

If they discovered his deception as a CID agent, any decision to deal with him might easily be reached.

He emptied his cup and turned to get a refill. If he hadn't been on close watch he might have missed the dusty, slow-moving SUV turning in off the highway and rolling across the front lot. He did note that it was missing license plates, and that alerted him instantly. The SUV came to a stop, sideways on to the motor court, and in line with Bolan's cabin. It sat, motor idling, faint heat waves shimmering above the hood. The windows were dark glass. The Executioner was unable to see in, but he had no doubt the occupants could see his room.

He put down his cup and turned to the bed, scooping up his weapons. The standard Beretta was back in his bag. He slid the 93-R into the shoulder holster, hefting the big .44 Magnum Desert Eagle. One in the chamber, eight in the magazine.

He looked back.

One of the SUV's rear doors swung open.

He saw the business end of an LAW missile launcher, laid across the shoulder of the man who emerged from the SUV, moving into position. The man cleared the vehicle and set himself to aim and fire.

Bolan was counting down the seconds as he turned and ran in the direction of the cabin's rear, aware that those seconds would be dropping fast. Legs powering, he covered the few yards to the back door, launching himself at the flimsy panel. The thin wood offered little resistance as Bolan's full-tilt impact struck it. He felt, rather than heard, the solid shock wave as the LAW missile detonated, blowing the cabin to matchsticks, filling the air with heat, smoke and splintered wood. His exit from the cabin was aided by the force of the blast as it caught him and hurled him across the dusty back lot. Bolan lost consciousness for long seconds, his body free of all tension, so that when he slammed down on the ground he took the impact without injury. When his dazed senses stopped cartwheeling and he was able to raise his head, he picked up the crackle of flames and the pattering fall of debris around him. He smelled scorching, as well. That came from his clothing. Pain rose through the dull ache that engulfed him. There was a stab of it across his left shoulder. Pushed by the Texas wind, acrid smoke fanned around him. Bolan struggled to his feet, swaying. His hearing had dulled from the blast.

Turning, he surveyed the burning ruin that had been his cabin and the first thought that cohered in his mind told him he'd been lucky not taking time to get that second cup of coffee.

He felt something in his right hand. He was still gripping the Desert Eagle. Bolan shoved it into his hip holster and pulled his jacket over it. He could taste blood in his mouth from a split lip. He raced away from the wreckage and crouched behind one of the other cabins. The wood down the side had been scorched by the blast. From where he was Bolan could see the front lot where the SUV had stood. The vehicle was gone.

The Executioner picked up distant sounds. He heard voices raised in alarm. He saw figures appearing from the dust and smoke. Someone saw him and pointed. Bolan recognized the guy from the diner, still wearing his cook's apron.

"Lord almighty, what the hell happened there, man?"

Bolan leaned against the cabin wall, weakness washing over him.

"Teach me to smoke in bed," he said, feeling his legs go.

"Griff, the man is hurt," a woman said. "Bleeding, too." It was the waitress from the diner. A tall, plain woman in her forties, she caught Bolan as he slumped against her. "Come on, boys, give the man a hand. Inside."

Bolan might have protested at any other time, but he hadn't the strength, or will, to resist. The day was already going gray around him, and before they reached the diner it had turned black.

"I HAVE YOU COVERED," Brognola said, his tone concerned. "What are these guys up to?" His displeasure was close to being a live thing, crackling through the cell phone in Bolan's hand.

Bolan understood his friend's difficult position when it came to these missions. Regardless of Stony Man Farm's presidential blessing, it was an ultracovert blessing and The Man still had ultimate sanctions. Bolan would not want to place either the president or Brognola under any pressure if a lone-wolf mission went sour. Not that he expected this one to. His intention was to make sure that OTG was shown to have been operating illegally and laying American military personnel open to risk by supplying defective equipment. If running that exposure identified members of the administration being in bed with Ordstrom, Bolan would welcome that, too. If he handed those people to the president that would be a bonus.

Until that happened Bolan was on his own. He had few people he could trust. Betrayal and violence would be working to stop him. The only people on his side were the people of Stony Man Farm, headed by Hal Brognola.

"Go talk to Sheriff Randall. I convinced him to keep a lid on this for the moment. He's pissed, but he's agreed to let you handle this the way you decide. Just don't go razing Macklin County to the ground, Striker," the big Fed said.

"My argument isn't with him. It's with those traitors out at Camp Macklin. Hal, thanks for the backup."

"Just tell me what's happening there."

Bolan explained the Camp Macklin scenario, ending with the LAW strike.

"Got to hand it to you, Striker. All these years on and you can still get people mad at you."

"That's the easy part," Bolan said. "Hal, how long can you cover my CID status? I need to get back inside the camp. They're rattled. I want to keep that going by showing up again tomorrow. If we do manage to keep a lid on this overnight, they won't be expecting me back."

"If anyone at the camp decides to check you out we can stall them. But Army CID has a long reach and we don't know how high up the corruption goes."

"Anything else to update me with?" Bolan asked.

"This goes deeper than even I thought," Brognola said. "Someone is covering for Ordstrom from inside the military. Any inquiries we make are being blocked. I can't get the time of day from some people. It's obvious orders are coming in from someone who doesn't want any connections with OTG to be looked at too closely."

"Sounds familiar."

"Doesn't it just."

"I'll be in touch."

"Watch your flank, Striker."

THE SAME SENTRY STEPPED OUT to check Bolan as he drew up at the gate the following morning. The moment he recognized Bolan the soldier saluted, then asked for ID. Bolan held back a smile. Corporal Huston handed back the ID wallet. He stared at the marks on Bolan's face.

"Begging the colonel's pardon, sir. Are you okay?"

"I'm fine, Corporal. It's just that they didn't tell me I had to wrestle my own steak out of the corral last night."

Huston took it in good humor, nodding conspiratorially at Bolan.

"You just go right ahead, Colonel."

Bolan parked outside the HQ building and went inside. He flashed his ID at the clerk, then made his way to Bosley's office and entered. Bosley glanced up, eyes widening as he recognized his visitor. There was a silent moment as he appraised Bolan. The Executioner witnessed the colonel's covert glance at the telephone on his desk.

"Stone, I guess yesterday didn't give you all the answers you expected," Bosley said, recovering reasonably well.

"I wouldn't say that, Colonel."

"So?"

"I need a little more time out on the testing ground."

"All you want, Colonel. I do believe Master Sergeant Randisi is on duty out there again."

"And Mr. Janssen?"

"He's over in the OTG facility armory."

"It's him I need to talk to first."

"Need a guide to take you there?"

"Spotted it on my way out to the testing range yesterday."

"Then I'll let you get on with your investigation," Bosley said, an unconcealed impatience in his tone.

Bolan walked from the HQ building. He rolled the car out along the camp road. As he drove he glanced in the rearview mirror and saw Colonel Bosley had followed him outside. The man appeared to be talking on a cell phone. Bolan found himself instinctively curious. It might have been nothing. Just a personal call. But why the need to take it outside? Away from the sanctum of his office? If anyone had privacy at Camp Macklin it would be Colonel Bosley. The thought began to chip away at Bolan's curiosity. He picked up his own cell phone from the seat beside him and hit a speed dial number, waiting while the electronic sequence went into action, sending the call up to a satellite, where it would be scrambled and rerouted finally to the Stony Man network.

"Striker, this must mean you need my help," Aaron "the Bear" Kurtzman said. "You never call to ask after my health."

"Good to hear your voice, too. Colonel Adam Bosley, commanding officer at Camp Macklin, Texas. I need all there is to know about the guy. ASAP."

The Bear grunted and Bolan imagined him shaking his great head. "One day you will ask for something that will give me a challenge, Striker. On that day I will rise from my wheelchair and walk again."

"Hell, I wish I could do that for you, pal."

"In the meantime I will tie one hand behind my back and take up your pitiful request. Call you back."

"If I'm busy just leave me a message." Bolan broke the connection and put the cell phone in his pocket.

A couple of minutes later the armory came into sight. It stood on its own, inside a chain-link-fence compound, some yards back from the road. The gates were open and Bolan spotted a civilian car parked near the building. It was Janssen's. There were no other vehicles in sight. Bolan rolled his car alongside Janssen's. He killed the engine and climbed out, reaching under his jacket to ease out the holstered Beretta. He held the weapon close to his right leg as he approached the armory entrance.

Bolan stepped inside, clearing the bright rectangle of the doorway, moving into shadow, the outer wall at his back. The building was long, wide, and had a high, curving roofline. It said military construction all the way down to the last rivet. Ahead of him Bolan saw rows of metal racking, each with numbers of shelves holding boxes and crates. More crates were stacked on the concrete floor. Somewhere within the building Bolan picked up the hum of air-conditioning units.

He picked up the faint rattle of movement far down the rows of racking—the scrape of shoe leather on the concrete. He heard the faintest creak of a distant door being opened, followed by the subdued sound of running feet.

Bolan turned and stood just inside the door, his eyes fixed on Janssen's car. He didn't have long to wait. The lean, tall figure of Stefan Janssen appeared around the end of the armory. He carried his suit jacket in his left hand as he moved in the direction of his parked car. Bolan could see the sweat glistening on Janssen's face. He waited until OTG's man pulled his keys from his pocket and aimed the remote at his car.

"Don't bother, Janssen. No time for running out just now. Stand where I can see you. Hands in sight."

Janssen pulled up short when he saw Bolan. He glanced in the direction of his waiting car, hope in his eyes.

"Not going to happen," Bolan said.

"You can't touch me," Janssen began, desperate to make it sound like a threat.

"Give it up, Janssen. You had your chance yesterday and screwed up. Now it's my turn. And I like the temperature just fine."

The fear in Janssen's eyes confirmed Bolan's suspicion about the failed rocket attack.

"I… What are you talking about? *What chance?*"

"The Sunbird Motor Court. They're one cabin down since I had that visit yesterday afternoon. That jog your memory?"

Janssen was unable to cover his complicity. "The hell with you, Stone. You've walked into something bigger than you ever figured." A sudden burst of confidence boosted his ego. "One call and you're history, Colonel. My employer can get you busted down to buck private."

"You still don't get it," Bolan said. "I don't give a damn. Ordstrom can't *touch* me. Here's something for you to think about. I'm not in the system. Civilian *or* military." Bolan moved his hand so Janssen could see the Beretta. "And this is all the backup I need."

Janssen became aware of his vulnerability. The man standing in front of him posed a *real* threat. One that was not bound by rules. "So who are you working for?"

Even as the words left Janssen's mouth his skull blew apart, filling the air with a hazy mist. The face dissolved as the heavy caliber projectile passed through, slamming into the armory wall beside him. A splash of blood and brains smeared the panel. As Janssen fell the distant bang of the shot reached Bolan's ears. He was already dropping to the ground, Janssen's shuddering corpse following him down.

Bolan crawled to the cover of Janssen's car, working his

way to the back so he could check out the near distance. From the position of the shot hitting Janssen he could assess a possible firing point. When he peered around the corner of the car he saw a military Humvee moving out of cover behind a stand of straggly brush. Dust coiled up from beneath the tires as the vehicle moved along the base road. It was traveling slowly, as if it was on a recon run.

Looking back over his shoulder Bolan checked out the hole in the armory wall. Big. It had punched through with ease.

He was thinking .50 caliber.

Army M-107 sniper rifle.

The specifications flashed through his mind. Eight-shot magazine. Effective range of 6,000 feet.

A powerful and deadly weapon in the hands of a skilled shooter.

Bolan recalled Master Sergeant Randisi's uniform displaying not just his rank, but the army sharpshooter badge. Bolan would have expected someone like Randisi to be a specialist in his field. The skilled soldier was capable of making the kind of shot that had just ended Janssen's life.

And now Bolan was a target on Randisi's home ground. Isolated. With little to back him up save the Beretta handgun he was carrying.

Bolan's fertile mind quickly reminded him he was not entirely defenseless. Directly behind him was the armory, where Janssen had been carrying out some business.

That store was holding an amount of military weaponry that might yet provide Bolan with a means of extracting himself from the current situation.

Staying flat, Bolan crawled away from the cover of the car and in through the armory door. Once inside, he pushed to his feet and searched the shelving racks for the weapon of his choice. He found what he wanted and snatched up a box of

M18 smoke canisters. Returning to the exit door Bolan peeled open the box and pulled out a couple of the canisters.

He saw the Humvee still moving in his direction, close enough now that he could see the driver behind the dusty windshield. As the vehicle turned sideways he recognized Randisi. Bolan realized the soldier was taking a calculated risk. Willing to go against Bolan despite the location. But Randisi was on home ground. The odds were in his favor. The armory was far enough from the main camp to allow Randisi some breathing space.

Bolan hadn't forgotten Colonel Bosley's odd behavior after their last meeting. The sudden cell phone call, away from the safety of his office. Bolan didn't dwell on that for too long. There would be time to dig into it later. Right now he had more pressing matters to handle.

The Executioner yanked out the pins from the first pair of canisters. He hurled the canisters over the roof of his parked car, in the general direction of Randisi's Humvee. As soon as the thick smoke began to erupt Bolan followed up with a couple more, spreading them so they formed a wide spill of dense smoke, obscuring the military vehicle, and more importantly hiding him from Randisi's sniper rifle. Bolan kept lobbing canisters as he broke from the armory door and lunged for his car. He slid onto the seat, turned the key to fire up the motor. He eased the car into gear, slammed his foot down and took the vehicle in a wide curve, tires burning. The car powered up and cruised through the compound gates, bursting through the thick bank of smoke and clearing the temporary cover. Ahead lay the camp road, snaking in the direction of the test range. Bolan hadn't intended to head in that direction, but with Randisi still a threatening presence he had little chance to make it back into the main camp. He hammered the gas pedal to the floor, feeling the car surge forward, pale dust swirling in his wake.

A glance in the rearview mirror showed the Humvee falling in behind, the dun-colored military vehicle accelerating quickly.

Randisi, it appeared, was not about to call it quits.

Neither was the Executioner.

7

Randisi was behind him, armed with the M-107. Bolan had his Beretta and his Desert Eagle. Handy weapons, but neither had the range or destructive power of the military rifle. Randisi could do his killing from a safe distance. Bolan needed to be up close and personal.

There were days, Bolan decided, when life took a perverse twist.

He checked out the terrain. The testing range had been situated on open, empty land, well away from the main camp, with nothing in any direction that might prove a possible risk to anyone. The isolation was another chosen factor. No one would be able to get close to the test area without being seen. Handy if people were up to no good.

Company was not expected, or encouraged. That left Bolan in the open, on his own, and unlikely to encounter anyone other than Randisi and any backup he might have.

It was a situation Bolan had been in on many occasions. He did not pass it off lightly, aware that it could prove to be a tricky extraction. But he took the position as he had always done, looking for the way out and operating with the same attitude he always employed. While he was able, he would resist. Resistance often presented its own results. Bolan was a realist and an optimist. He viewed nothing as hopeless. There was always a way out of any struggle. It sometimes took a little longer to find the exit, that was all.

The Humvee was closing fast. The uneven surface of the dirt road was easier for the military vehicle. The wide tire span handled the ruts and undulations with ease. Bolan's car was designed for smoother surfaces and while it was by no means having problems, the rough track was hammering at the suspension, causing some lack of traction. Bolan was having to control the steering wheel, too, as it rocked under his grip.

A large shadow darkened the road just ahead. Bolan leaned forward to peer through the windshield and saw the camouflaged underside of a Bell Huey military chopper. The helicopter ran ahead of his car, then dipped, the landing skids almost touching the hood of the vehicle. The pilot was good, keeping the chopper on an even keel just ahead of the car, causing Bolan to ease off the gas pedal. As he slowed, the Humvee grew larger in the mirror. The Executioner felt it slam into the back of his car. The impact jolted him forward. He felt the rear of the car lift, then drop again with a solid thump.

He saw the metal landing skid of the helicopter a second before it hit the windshield. The glass cracked. Bolan jerked the wheel and the car swerved violently to the left, away from the bulk of the Huey. The roar of the Humvee's motor rose as it surged forward again. The solid impact, catching the car corner on, flipped it on its side. Bolan was slammed against the driver's door, the impact driving breath from his body. His side of the car was against the ground, the window shattered. Dust and debris blew in through the gap. He felt the sudden explosion as the air bag inflated, pinning him against the seat back. The car was struck again, sending it in a dizzy spin. Bolan's senses were thrown off-kilter. His world became a kaleidoscope of sound and color. There was little he could do, hampered by the pressure of the air bag and the movement of the car. He felt the sudden jolt as something slammed against the top edge of the car's roof. He felt the car rocking. More thumps, the car swaying, then there was a distinct dropping motion. Bolan felt the car slam to a stop. The motion sent him into a dizzying fade and nothing seemed to make sense….

When awareness came drifting back, Bolan felt disoriented, his body aching from the impact. He could hear the steady beat of heavy sound close by. It took him a moment to realize it had come from the Huey's spinning rotors. He fought against the confines of the air bag. Only then did he recognize he was sitting more or less upright. The car was back on its wheels. Dark shadows on his left moved in and out of his hazy vision. The driver's door was wrenched open, hands reaching inside to drag him out of the car. When he resisted, hard fists slammed into his face and body. Bolan struggled to fight back. His coordination had not yet returned and he was helpless against being hauled from the car, dragged across the dusty ground. He became highly aware of the Huey's spinning rotors. His vision cleared long enough for him to make out the bulk of the chopper before he was dragged up into the passenger compartment. He was dumped on the ribbed decking, face against the cold metal. Around him the Huey vibrated, sound filling his ears, the familiar odors of fuel and hot oil searing his nostrils. Figures moved around him. He heard someone yelling. The chopper powered up, shuddered, then began to rise off the ground.

Air gusted in through the open side hatch. It pulled at Bolan's clothing, slapped his face and pulled him out of the hazy state that gripped him. He called on reserves of strength to get him back on his feet, knowing that if he didn't he was not going to come out of this very well. His only avenue of escape was in forcing the matter to his own advantage. He cracked one eye, checking out the situation as the chopper began to bank.

He saw Randisi braced against the soft pitch and roll of the chopper, one hand gripping a Beretta. He was in some heated exchange with Colonel Bosley, ignoring any pretense at recognizing the other's rank.

"That was a bonehead move. Using a fucking LAW to take out one guy. You even screwed that up. We should have done what I said and offed the son of a bitch first day he showed. Kept it on base."

"And what if he had been a genuine military cop? We would have had the whole damn corps swarming over us," Bosley said.

"Not if we'd done it carefully. But you had to go and advertise it across the fucking state of Texas."

"Then let's do it now. Put a bullet in the head and dump him."

"Jesus, Bosley, it's so plain you've never seen combat."

"What?"

"All you want to do is go around shooting everybody."

"What do you call putting a fifty caliber into Janssen?"

"Insurance. That civilian pussy would have told everything he knew."

Bosley grunted something unintelligible. He swung around, driving a savage kick in Bolan's direction. The blow failed to land as Bolan turned his body aside, then hauled himself up off the chopper's deck and launched himself into Bosley. The colonel gasped as Bolan's solid bulk struck. He lost control and stumbled back across the compartment, colliding with Randisi. Bolan followed up fast, his eyes on the Beretta in Randisi's fist. He made a grab for the man's wrist, caught it and yanked the master sergeant toward him, sledging his free hand around. Bolan's fist slammed into Randisi's mouth, and blood spurted from his split lips. Bosley, still partially caught between the struggling men, dragged his body free, then lashed out, catching Bolan across the shoulder. The Executioner slammed Randisi's gun hand into the metal bulkhead. The Beretta hung from Randisi's trigger finger. Bolan made a grab for it, closing his own hand over the pistol, swinging it to hammer into Randisi's face. He struck hard, a number of times. He opened bloody gashes that leaked into Randisi's eyes as the man slumped to his knees. Bolan jerked his knee into Randisi's jaw, driving the man facedown on the deck.

Feeling Bosley still slamming his fist against his shoulder Bolan half turned and drove a hard fist into the man's soft gut. Bosley choked, his grip slackening. Bolan grabbed his shirt and swung Bosley around, throwing him across the compartment. The colonel grunted as he slammed into the bulkhead. Bolan landed a couple more blows that shocked Bosley's system. In desperation Bosley launched himself forward, hands reaching out to claw at Bolan's face. Bolan eased back, slapping aside Bosley's hands. As the man stepped back Bolan raised his right foot and planted it against Bosley's torso, pushing hard. Bosley backpedaled, arms flailing, and made a failed attempt to steady himself. He half turned, stepping back too far, his left foot meeting thin air as he reached the edge of the deck. He clawed for a handhold that wasn't there and as the slipstream caught him he vanished from sight through the open hatch. His hoarse scream was lost in the chatter of the chopper's engines.

Coming up off the deck, Randisi hit Bolan with everything he had, hard fists and solid knees, driving the Executioner back across the compartment. As the bulkhead stopped him short Bolan reversed the Beretta and slammed the butt down on Randisi's skull with all the remaining strength he could muster. Randisi fell to his knees, then went facedown on the deck plating.

Bolan remained against the bulkhead, waiting for the waves of nausea to pass.

Despite his physical condition Bolan had the presence of mind to keep the Beretta trained on the Huey's young pilot. The helmeted man had twisted around in his seat as the struggle had taken place. Seeing that Bolan was in command, the pilot concentrated on flying, keeping his face turned away.

"Let's keep it that way, son," Bolan said. "All I want is for you to turn this chopper around and take us back."

"What about the colonel?"

"Bosley took his chance. Turned out to be the wrong one, but that isn't my problem. Just take me back to where I left my car."

"Is Randisi all right?"

"Remains to be seen, soldier. Right now I've got other things to worry about."

Bolan stayed where he could watch the pilot as the Huey swung around and headed on its return journey. His thoughts were moving ahead, assessing his need to locate and protect Frank Carella. The former OTG man was out on his own, unable to figure who he could trust and in possession of material that would blow Ordstrom's illegal dealing clear out of the water. With the high stakes involved, Ordstrom and his security team would be desperate to bring the situation back under control. That desperation was starting to show itself, which was why Bosley and Randisi had made their play. Getting rid of him would have been an ideal solution. With the collapse of the Camp Macklin opposition Bolan would have Ordstrom back on his tail with a vengeance. Bolan had to stay ahead of the man while searching for Carella.

His priority was getting clear of Camp Macklin. He doubted that the whole of the base was in with Bosley and Randisi, but there was no way he was going to identify who was and who wasn't. His safest option was to leave the camp and clear out of Texas, moving back east to start tracking Carella. Bolan's visit to the Lone Star State had forced OTG's hand, exposing the setup at Macklin. Bolan would let the authorities move in to clean out the viper's nest while he went after bigger game.

He felt the chopper start to descend. Leaning out the side hatch, he saw his wrecked car beside Randisi's Humvee. He felt the skids touch down.

"Cut the power, soldier." Bolan waited until the Huey closed down. "Step out. Walk twenty yards ahead so I can see you."

The pilot climbed out and removed his helmet. He was young, almost too young, Bolan thought.

"I heard you were from Army CID," the pilot said. "What's going on, Colonel?"

"You'll hear soon enough. Now walk, soldier, that's an order."

Bolan waited until the pilot had reached his designated spot, then climbed back inside the Huey, where he ripped out a handful of cables, disabling the helicopter. He also put the chopper's radio out of action. He checked Randisi. The man was still unconscious, breathing steadily. He was going to have the mother of all headaches when he woke up. Bolan left the man where he was. He made his way to the rental car and located his weapons. He opened the trunk and retrieved his bag. The Executioner went to the Humvee and climbed in, firing up the motor. He swung the heavy combat vehicle around and headed back in the direction of the main camp. If he could clear the camp and reach the main highway his immediate problems might ease.

Bolan had forgotten about his cell phone. It caught him off guard when it rang. He took it out of his pocket.

"Yeah?"

"You sound a little aggrieved, big guy," Kurtzman said.

"It's been one of those days," Bolan said. "Kind of up and down."

"I have information."

"Tell me it's about Colonel Bosley and how he has cash accounts stashed away."

Kurtzman grumbled under his breath. "Why do I bother if you already know?"

"It came to me after we spoke. Kind of in a roundabout way."

"Is the colonel busted?"

"You could say that," Bolan said.

"What is this, Striker, cryptic riddle day?"

"Can you trace Bosley's benefactor?"

"On it as we speak. I have information for you about Frank Carella. His only living relative is a sister. Veronica. She lives in Billings, Montana. I have the full address if you haven't already plucked it out of the ether."

"I need to call you back," Bolan said as he approached the main camp. "Right now I have to work my way out of a situation."

He clicked off the phone and dropped it back in his pocket. Bolan reached for his ID. He drove the Humvee along the base main road, keeping his speed down and his eyes ahead. He followed the road until he saw the main gate ahead, bringing the Humvee to a halt at the barrier. He sat waiting until Corporal Huston finished a phone call. The man stepped out and bent to check out the Humvee's driver.

"Colonel?" Huston couldn't have failed to spot the dusty suit and the blood on Bolan's face. "You look worse than when you came in. You need any help?"

"Under control, Corporal. Something came up relating to my inquiry. It's being handled. I need to rendezvous with CID agents coming in right now. This is priority, Huston. And I need you to contact the base second in command. Have him handle this. He'll need to check out Master Sergeant Randisi and the OTG liaison." Bolan's voice rose hard. "Do it, Corporal. And get that barrier up. At the double."

Huston stepped back, reacting to Bolan's orders. He thumbed the button and the steel barrier rose. Bolan drove through, maintaining a slow speed, only picking up the pace once he was clear. The quarter mile to the main highway seemed much longer. Bolan hit the highway and swung the Humvee in the direction of the Macklin County airport.

So far, so good, he thought.

He knew that the game was far from over. Even if he had exposed the Camp Macklin players, the conspiracy was not going to roll over and play dead. There was far too much at stake, too many important people involved. They would be scrambling to reposition by now. Each one doing his best to cover his tracks. Consolidating. Protecting. Attempting to isolate themselves from any potential fallout. Bolan smiled at the images. It was what he liked about these deals. Once the foundations had been shaken, the rats started to scurry for cover. And it was during these times that mistakes were made.

He kept checking behind him, half expecting to see vehicles in hot pursuit. Camp Macklin would be buzzing once the recent events were exposed. Bolan took out his phone and called Brognola. He related what had happened at the camp.

"We know Colonel Bosley and Master Sergeant Randisi were involved. They had a guy from OTG on site. Janssen. Their contact. I didn't get anything from him before Randisi put a .50-caliber bullet into his skull to shut him up."

Bolan hit the brakes, bringing the Humvee to a sliding halt. He climbed from the vehicle and went to the back. Leaning inside, he opened one of the metal equipment lockers. Inside was the M-107 Randisi had used to silence Janssen.

"Striker, you still there?" the big Fed said.

"I'm here, Hal. You'll need to get it checked out, but I have a feeling I'm looking at the rifle that was used to shoot Francis Nelson. Same one Randisi used to shoot the OTG guy, Janssen. If you can get the bullets checked don't be surprised if they turn out to match."

8

The Virginia darkness had become a double-edged sword, promising anonymity but also hiding possible threats. As far as Frank Carella was concerned, he anticipated trouble and expected little in assurance. More than once he asked himself why he had accepted Cal Ryan's summons to this isolated place. It left him uneasy, wary of every sound and the overlapping shadows that could easily hide a man. He understood Ryan's concerns and why he had chosen this place. But he still felt vulnerable.

Their discovery, capable of bringing Jacob Ordstrom and his company to its knees, had left both men open to harm. Carella knew how ruthless Ordstrom could be. OTG was his life. He ran the vast corporation with a hard hand. Nothing could stand in its way. No threat to its sanctity would be tolerated.

Now that Ryan and Carella had taken this initial step, there would be no going back. Ordstrom would know they were willing to blow his conspiracy wide open. There was incriminating evidence that could not be denied.

There was no turning back. Commitment was a one-way street.

Carella felt a chill that had nothing to do with the low temperature. He would be the first to admit he was scared. He was no hero. Just an ordinary guy trying to do the right thing. No one had ever suggested that doing the right thing might turn out to be so risky.

He heard the sound of a car engine. Low, the vehicle moving

slowly. Tires crunching over rough ground. Carella turned and picked out the dark shape of the car. It was running without lights. It came to a stop. Sat silently as the motor was cut.

Carella stayed put, watching the car. He couldn't make out color, or even model, so he couldn't even be sure it was Ryan. His cell, on vibrate mode, alerted him to an incoming call. Carella flipped it open.

"You around?" Ryan asked.

"Is that you in the car, Cal?"

"It's me. Where are you?" Ryan's voice sounded strained.

"Twenty feet in front of you."

"Stay put, I'm coming over."

"Make it quick, Cal, I have a bad feeling about this place."

The driver's door opened and a dark shape emerged. As the figure made its way across to where Carella stood he leaned forward, trying to identify Ryan. He breathed easier when he recognized his friend. That feeling vanished at the warning expression in Ryan's eyes. Ryan shook his head, only slightly, the briefest warning he could give his friend. His face was a pale blur as he suddenly opened his mouth to speak.

"A trap...go."

Carella looked beyond Ryan, back to the car. He caught the merest flicker of movement.

The unexpected crack of a gun startled him. The sound was harsh in the surrounding quiet. Then a second shot, the scant glare of the muzzle blast.

Ryan was flung forward, expelling a hoarse cry as he stumbled and fell to his knees.

"Go!"

Carella stepped back. He could see two dark shapes emerging from behind Ryan's car. He found himself turning, willing his legs to move. Fear rose. The sound of another shot. He jerked aside and felt the low branches of the trees catch his face.

The trees.

They would give him cover. Hide him from…*from who?* Ordstrom's people? They were the only ones he could imagine being behind this attack. He had no desire to confirm that.

His mind burned with questions. Too many with no answers. As he ran, Carella decided that now was not the time to dwell on such things. His priority was to get away—to stay alive.

The rattle of more gunshots added to his resolve. Bullets whipped through the trees, chunking into bark, shredding leaves on the lower branches.

Jesus, he thought, they really mean it.

The bastards were trying to kill him. They had just killed Ryan. He was certain his friend was dead. And all because he and Carella had uncovered some unsavory information.

He caught his foot against an exposed root and almost fell. Flinging out his arms, he felt the rough bark of a tree. He gripped it to hold himself up. His face slammed against the trunk, the rough bark scraping the flesh of his right cheek. He reacted to the stinging pain, pushed away from the tree and picked up his stride again. Overhead a pale moon cleared the clouds and he gained some illumination, the cold light spearing down through the trees to show him a glimmer of the way ahead. The small consolation of that was tempered by the fact that the same light would also aid his pursuers.

The ground fell away in a steep slope. Carella plunged down, regardless of any possible risk to himself. The imagined sensation of a bullet striking him simply added to his speed. Carella went to his knees as the slope leveled out and he slithered for some feet before he was able to control his fall. Back on his feet, sucking air into his starved lungs, the desperate man angled off to the left and followed the uneven ground, heading deeper into the heavy stand of timber and brush, ignoring the clutching drag of thorny strands against his clothes. He concentrated on maintaining some distance from his attackers. Sweat trickled down his face, stinging harshly in the scratches on his cheek. The pain concentrated his mind, forcing him to keep moving. Sooner or later he was going to reach the place where the trees gave way to the highway. If he could get that far and pick up a taxi…

Another round of shots blasted through the night. They were closing in on him. The shots went wide, the closest ripping off a chunk of bark from a slender trunk, exposing pale wood beneath. Close or not, it told Carella his pursuers had not given up the chase.

It would have been so easy to give up. To let his pursuers catch up and end it. He could hand over the flash drives and let it end there and then. Carella's mind was playing tricks. He realized that. It was fear and exhaustion adding to his panic. His sudden grasp of the situation made him snap out of it. He thought of his friend Cal Ryan doing his best to warn Carella and getting himself shot for his trouble. He couldn't allow Ryan's sacrifice to have happened for nothing. Carella wasn't that much of a defeatist.

He pushed on and crashed through the thick undergrowth. He wasn't even sure which way he was going now. Because of that he failed to see the drop-off. It was only when one foot met thin air that he realized. It was too late. He pitched forward, arms swinging, and dropped. He hit the slope below, landing hard. Breath burst from his lungs, the impact stunning him into silence and shock. He barely felt his downward flight as he bounced and crashed to the deep bottom. He landed hard, head slamming into the ground, and the dark night went even darker as he slithered into the tangled brush that covered the bottom of the gulley. He lay close to unconsciousness, partly submerged in the swift-moving stream that wound its way along the base of the deep trench. He drifted in and out of awareness, too stunned to react to the sound of his pursuers as they scoured the area, missing the drop-off by yards. The noisy sound of their passing eventually faded, leaving only silence.

Carella lay where he had fallen, drifting in and out of consciousness. He slipped into an exhausted sleep. When he finally woke, becoming aware of his surroundings, dawn had already broken. He lay for some time, feeling coming back. He was aching from head to toe, his body stiff and cold. Dragging himself out of the water he saw that he was soaked from the waist down. Carella sat up, scooping water up to douse his face, wincing against the pain from his battered face.

He recalled with a start the reason why he was here. He remembered the events of the previous night. The armed men. The shooting of his friend Ryan. He dropped to the ground again and took a long look around. Nothing. There was no sound, either, except for the local wildlife. Through the canopy formed by the trees he could see the sky. Blue. Cloudless. Empty.

He had escaped the search because he had fallen down into the deep gulley, hidden by the dark and thick foliage. Somehow his pursuers had overlooked him. Carella didn't think for one minute that they would give up on him. There were other places they could look. His apartment. His girlfriend's home. His sister. She lived in Montana. Would they look that far away? Carella knew the answer. *They would.* Hadn't they gunned down Ryan? Killed Francis Nelson? That alone proved how desperate they were to get their hands on the information Carella had on him.

He stayed where he was for a while, letting his body recover. Slowly he walked about, easing the kinks from his limbs. Overhead the heat of the sun filtered down through the trees and warmed him. Finally he started along the winding course of the gully, searching for a way out. He had to get clear. There were things he needed to do. Warn his sister. His girlfriend. His concern for them gnawed at his conscience. His actions were liable to place them both in danger. If anything happened to them…

He needed to find a telephone. A public phone. He daren't use his cell because he was experiencing feelings of paranoia. He understood that even cell phone calls could be traced and his personal number was on file at OTG. That would have been one of the first things Arnold Hoekken would have initiated. That and his home phone and his computer. They would have everything covered. Carella realized he would be tracked by any of those items. OTG would isolate him, leaving him helpless. At their mercy. He knew that Ordstrom had influence that reached as far as military and government sources. Who else did he have on his payroll? Law enforcement? FBI?

Carella shook with fear. He was fast becoming an outsider. Unable to trust anyone, because they might have—however tenuous—links that could run all the way back to Ordstrom. Damn the man. Damn his power, his influence, the insidious length of his reach.

He had no idea how long he walked through the forest. When he checked his watch he saw it must have been an hour or more. Suddenly he came on a trail winding its way cross-country. He joined it, moving on, hoping he might find some kind of habitation. He was hopelessly lost. There was no way he could have located where he had parked his car the previous night.

Carella checked his pocket. He located his cell phone, tempted to use it. He held it in his dirt-encrusted hand, staring at it. Then he switched it off and shoved it back in his pocket. Patting his stained jacket he felt the bulge of his wallet. He checked it. Cash. A number of credit cards. Not much use at the moment. But maybe they would be if he planned his next moves carefully.

Thinking about his girlfriend, Lesley, had generated something that might provide the answer to his immediate problem. He needed somewhere to hide while he figured out how to save himself and also get the information he held into the hands of the right people. And thinking about Lesley reminded him of a place they both knew that could allow him some breathing space.

First he needed to get clear of the area. Well clear. He needed to do it fast. Before Ordstrom's people pinpointed him again. To achieve that he had to get his hands on more money.

It took him almost two hours to reach the main highway. Heading back in the direction of the city he finally flagged down a passing car and got a ride to the first available gas station. The car driver made no comment on Carella's appearance, happy enough to talk endlessly about the benefits of the insurance policies he was selling.

9

Bolan spotted the man watching Carella's apartment building as he crossed the street, heading for the entrance. Too obvious. Whoever he was, the watcher had little experience at remaining invisible. Bolan let the man pick him up and tail him. He kept moving, up the stairs to Carella's floor. The watcher followed, remaining a flight back, but staying with his subject.

Turning along the corridor, Bolan made his way to Carella's door. He used his picks to gain entrance, closed the door behind him and stood for a few moments in the shadowed hall, checking the layout, then moved on through the apartment. It was small but well furnished. Carella had spent time and thought on the layout. He had also indulged himself by having a number of framed photographs of an attractive young woman placed in strategic positions around the living area and the bedroom. A couple of them had been signed Lesley. When Bolan checked Carella's telephone log there were calls from someone with the same name. He went through the drawers of the desk standing under the main window and found Carella's book listing phone numbers and addresses. There was an entry for Lesley Cornwell, with an address across town. Bolan slid the slim notebook into his jacket pocket and turned to complete his search of the apartment.

He was crossing the hall when he picked up sounds beyond the apartment door. When he checked he saw the door handle moving as someone tested it. The Executioner moved to one side of the door as it began to open. He let the intruder get his head and shoulders inside, then reached out and caught hold of the guy's coat, yanking him through the door. Bolan threw the man along the hallway. The intruder lost his balance and slammed facedown on the carpet. Bolan kicked the door shut.

The guy on the carpet was already rising to his feet, reaching under his coat for a slim-bladed knife sheathed on his belt. The cold steel blade was thrust in Bolan's direction.

"I should'a done you earlier, chummy."

Bolan recognized a rough British accent. The lean, bony-faced opponent brushed thick, dark blond hair away from his eyes, his wide lips pulling back in a confident grin. He lunged at Bolan, the keen blade of the knife springing forward in his hand. The flat edge slid across the leather sleeve of Bolan's jacket as he sidestepped. His agility surprised his attacker. The Brit stepped lightly on his feet, performing a springy dance as he weaved back and forth, then sucked in his breath and made a second lunge. Bolan sensed the feint for what it was and instead of pulling away this time he walked inside the guy's moving arm. The Brit had been anticipating a swift follow-up, intended to catch Bolan off guard. He was countered before he could recover. Bolan clamped the man's wrist with his left hand, pushed the knife aside, then drove his bunched fist into the guy's face with all the strength he could muster. The blow rocked the Brit, snapping his head back with considerable force.

Without a pause Bolan encircled the Brit's arm, levered hard and snapped the bone below the elbow. The guy howled in pain. The knife slid from numb fingers, landing point first on the carpeted floor. Bolan slammed a shoulder into the guy's chest, propelling him backward, the impact taking the man off his feet. He crashed down on a glass-topped coffee table. The table shattered under the weight, showering glass and splintered wood over the Brit.

The man rolled over, ignoring the shards of glass slicing into his hands. He was breathing hard, favoring the broken arm, but he still moved fast. Gathering himself, he made a lunge for the knife he had dropped, grasping it with his good hand and powering to his feet. He sank into a semicrouch, the blade of the knife arcing back and forth.

"Come and get it, mate. I'm going to enjoy this."

Impatience made the Brit move in, his left-handed lunge awkward. Bolan avoided him easily, then blocked the knife arm. He pushed it up and back. He slammed his left elbow into the Brit's face, stunning the man. Bolan yanked the knife from the dazed man's fingers and thrust it deeply into the exposed neck, slicing the main artery. As Bolan stepped back the guy sank to his knees, blood already starting to pump out around the knife blade. The Brit reached up to pull the knife free, but his strength was fading.

As the guy toppled facedown on the bloody carpet, Bolan stepped back, reaching beneath his jacket for the holstered Beretta in case the knife man had any backup close by. He moved to the door and opened it cautiously. The corridor beyond was deserted. He put away the Beretta and closed the apartment door. He made his way downstairs and out onto the street. The Executioner returned to where he had parked the rental car and slid behind the wheel.

He had to give Ordstrom credit for keeping his teams on the move and covering the ground. Whoever was running the strike teams was not leaving anything to chance. Going on what he had already seen, he knew the opposition would find Carella's girlfriend pretty soon. The Executioner knew that he had to get to her quickly.

10

"You understand what I'm telling you? What might happen if you let yourself become involved?"

"Frank, I understand. Now stop changing the subject and tell me how you are."

"You mean how scared am I? How I wish I hadn't seen that damned deleted file. Right now my life is not what I would choose it to be. Apart from that I'll see a lot of the country. I'll get a nice tan and grow a beard."

"Jesus, Frank, stop making light of this."

She heard him suck in his breath. "Lesley, if I didn't I would most likely wait for the next train and lay my head on the track."

Lesley Cornwell realized how insensitive her remark must have seemed. The man was alone, by his own admission, scared, and was trying to maintain a semblance of sanity. And there she was deriding his mood.

"I'm sorry, Frank. Just like me to step in it with both feet. It must be terrible. I won't even try to understand what you're going through. Please, tell me what I can do to help. And do not say there's nothing I can do. You know how I feel about you."

Her final words almost made her lose her grip. She forced herself to control her emotions. Frank needed support. They both had to remain calm.

"It's because of how we feel I'm reluctant to get you caught up in this. Everything that's happened has made me realize how desperate Ordstrom is to suppress those files. If he suspects you've even talked to me he'll come after you, too."

"Listen to me, love. Why can't you send me the information and I'll get it to the right people. Once it's out in the open there won't be any need for Ordstrom to want you hurt. He'll be too busy trying to stay out of jail."

"No, I'm not going to put you in the firing line. And don't argue. It's not debatable. I have to work this out my own way. One of the problems is deciding who I can trust with this information now that Cal is dead."

"Doesn't that tell you how dangerous this all is? First Francis. Now Cal. It's a nightmare. How can you think straight while you're on the run? It's a no-win situation. Frank, honey, I want you back with me. Safe and well and not ducking for cover every time someone knocks on the door."

"I want the same, but it isn't going to happen until I get this mess sorted."

"Just tell me where you are."

"So you can come charging down here to rescue me? Not going to happen. You need to stay away."

She knew this was an argument she could not win. Though she understood his reluctance to involve her, she still wanted to be with him. He mattered to her. More than she might have realized until this moment.

"Please be careful, Frank."

"I will," he said.

She heard some background noise. Faint, but recognizable. About to speak, she checked herself. She didn't want to put him on his guard by telling him she knew where he was. Instead she repeated her warning that he be careful.

"Call when it's safe," she said softly. "I love you, Frank Carella."

Lesley put down the receiver, slumped back in her seat. She

stared at the wall above the telephone, not even registering the fact that the framed picture there was hanging crookedly.

Puerto Laredo.

That was where he was. She had no doubt. The background noise she had picked up established and confirmed his whereabouts.

The quiet Mexican coastal town on Mexico's Baja Peninsula, nestled around the harbor that gave its name to the spot, where she and Carella had spent a number of vacations. Not quite isolated, but certainly not on the main tourist map. The kind of place to go when you didn't want to be found. Lesley should have guessed it would be Carella's destination.

She made her way to the kitchen and made herself a mug of coffee. Leaning against the breakfast bar, she tried to work out if anyone else knew about Puerto Laredo. They had never really talked about the place to anyone, realizing that if they revealed the location of their favorite spot, others might show up. So Puerto Laredo had remained a secret. *Their* secret, and Lesley wanted it to stay that way. But that might change now. If Ordstrom's people found out, Puerto Laredo might become Carella's nightmare.

The sound of her door chimes startled her. Her hand shook and she spilled coffee on the breakfast bar. She stared at the brown liquid, wondering if it might stain if she didn't clean it up.

The chimes sounded again, almost taking on an insistent tone.

Lesley placed the mug down and made her way across the apartment.

"Who is it?"

The moment she had asked the question, the thought entered her head that never, ever before had she asked visitors that question. There had never been a need before. Some of Frank's nervousness had transferred to her. Under normal circumstances she was a strong-willed young woman, not given to panic or unease. Right now she was exhibiting both those traits. She didn't like the sensation, and she felt herself getting angry.

"Well, are you going to tell me who you are?" she called out.

"Miss Cornwell, my name is Matt Cooper, and I need to talk with you urgently."

The voice was firm, without menace. The words were delivered in a steady tone.

"I don't know you, Mr. Cooper. Why should I listen to you?"

"Because I'm looking for Frank Carella and you might know where he is."

Lesley stepped away from the door, fear rising in her. She looked back at the telephone sitting on the small table, almost as if it might give her an answer. She had only been talking to Frank moments ago and now someone was at her door asking about him.

"Miss Cornwell, I'm not the enemy. If I was I'd be battering down your door, not standing here talking to you through it."

"Easy to say. I let you in, then what happens? What if I said I was going to pick up the phone and call the police?"

"I'd say you were thinking with your head. Lesley, Frank is in danger. The people looking for him are not going to be as nice as me. They've already killed someone else involved and I believe they may try to get to Frank through you. If you feel you need to speak to the police, go ahead. I'll wait out here until they arrive. Just remember that the longer you delay the more time you give to the men looking for Frank."

Lesley reached out to unlock the door, paused, then made her decision and freed the catch. She stepped away from the door, ready to...*to what?* Her mind raced as she tried to decide what she would do if the man outside threatened her. She was no coward. Often called too determined, the sheer strength of her personality was enough to take her through any situation. She hoped it would work for her this time.

"The door's unlocked, Mr. Cooper."

The man who stepped into the apartment was tall. Over six feet. Thick black hair. Good-looking in an unassuming way. He carried his strong physique well. He looked to be a confident man, she decided. There was an expression in his blue eyes that made her feel comfortable. She noticed, too, the marks on his face that hadn't been left by careless shaving.

"Would you like me to leave the door open?" Bolan asked. "If it makes you feel safer."

She felt the corners of her mouth turn up slightly at his remark. What was it about him that left her feeling unthreatened?

"Who are you, Mr. Cooper?" She stepped forward and closed the door, then turned to face him. "And how are you involved in this?"

"I went to a funeral recently. Watched a man bury his son. Francis Nelson. His father is Colonel Dane Nelson. He asked me to look into his son's death because he believes he died investigating irregularities that originated at OTG. Frank works at OTG. Nelson told me his son and a journalist named Cal Ryan were in contact about corruption at OTG. Frank knew Ryan and Francis Nelson. It appears he found similarly incriminating data at OTG. He and Ryan were going to pool what they'd found. I just learned that Ryan is dead. Shot to death. I believe Frank is on the run. He doesn't trust anyone. Doesn't know where to turn. But you already know this, Lesley. I think you're smart enough to know that Jacob Ordstrom is a very powerful man. He has the contacts and the influence to keep Frank out in the cold until his people track him down. I don't want that to happen."

"Let's assume you're telling me the truth, Mr. Cooper. Just how do you figure on protecting Frank? I mean just who do *you* represent? How many people do you have behind you?"

"There's just me," Bolan told her.

"One man?" Lesley's expression revealed her disbelief.

"Tell me you don't wear blue tights and a red cape under your street clothes?"

"It doesn't always take a team. Less is sometimes better."

The young woman regarded him intently. Bolan returned her stare, deciding that Frank Carella was a lucky man. He could see why he had her photographs all around his apartment. Not only was she attractive, but she was also smart and plainly capable of holding her own.

"Can we sit down?" he asked. "It's been a busy day."

"Oh, why not. Hey, would you like coffee?"

Bolan said he would and took a seat on the leather couch. He watched as Lesley crossed to the kitchen area and busied herself.

"I knew Francis," she said. "He was a nice guy. How long did you know him?"

"I didn't. But what happened to him was wrong. I promised his father his death wouldn't be in vain."

"Are you a private eye?" Lesley asked.

Bolan shrugged. "No. Do I look like one?"

"On TV they're always getting beaten up, too."

Bolan touched a bruised cheek. "You noticed."

"Hard not to. Did you get those bruises because of this business?"

"Yes."

She brought their mugs of coffee, then sat in an armchair facing Bolan.

"I know you're not a plumber. Or a delivery man, Mr. Cooper, so just *what* are you?"

"That isn't important right now. Let's just say I have the means to do this job. And drop the mister. Call me Cooper."

Lesley sipped at her coffee. Bolan saw her eyes widen. She leaned forward, staring, and he realized she had spotted the Beretta in the shoulder rig, exposed where his leather jacket had gaped.

"Tool of the trade," Bolan explained.

"Must be a tough business you're in, Cooper."

"I don't promote needlepoint."

"I should hope not, with a selling aid like that." She drew her gaze from the holstered weapon. "For the sake of argument, if I did know where Frank was, how could you help him?"

"Ordstrom needs to prevent the information Frank has from becoming public. If it gets into safe hands OTG is in deep trouble. The revelation that OTG is party to fraudulently supplying defective equipment to the military would bring down a large house of cards. There have to be others involved. Individuals in the military and within the business sector. There's bound to be big money floating around from this fraud. Once the information is aired there'll be panic. Everyone in the game will be covering their tracks. Denying involvement. Pointing the fingers to put the heat on anyone but themselves. I need to get Frank to someone I know who can make sure his evidence gets seen by the right people. The more people who see it, the better for Frank."

"*If* you can pull it off, Cooper."

Bolan drank his coffee. "I can," he said.

"You said Ordstrom's people already tried to kill someone else?"

"Dane Nelson. They made an attempt on his way back home from his son's funeral. They didn't succeed."

"Was he hurt?"

"Took a bullet in the shoulder. His driver was badly wounded."

"This is hard to believe. What about the men who attacked them?"

"They didn't make it."

She gave him a solemn look, realization dawning.

"*You* were there?" Bolan only nodded. "Why did they want to hurt him?"

"As Francis's father he would be considered a threat. Any threat has to be taken down."

"What kind of people are these? There's no justification for indiscriminate murder, Cooper."

"We're dealing with dangerous people, Lesley. Ruthless men prepared to go to extreme lengths to protect themselves."

Bolan saw her slump back in the chair, her scared eyes moving back and forth around the room. He realized that for her this was a view into a different world from the one she normally inhabited. She was looking into Mack Bolan's world. It was new and frightening and he understood her reaction.

"Can you help Frank?"

"I'll do whatever it takes."

"But you can't promise he might not get hurt? Even killed?"

"On his own he most likely will die if Ordstrom's people find him. Give me the opportunity and I'll give him a fighting chance."

"Jesus, what a choice. I put him at risk however I answer. Cooper, you make it hard for a girl."

Bolan had no glib answer for that. He understood, because he was presenting her with a difficult decision. But there was no other way. No simple, clean way to resolve the situation. If there had been, he would have taken it without hesitation. But Ordstrom's hard men would not be considering any gentle ways of persuasion. Their way was to go straight for the heart. Do whatever was needed to gain their goal, and it didn't matter in the slightest who got hurt in the process. They trampled over everything. Cut down what stood in their way. They were destroyers, violators.

The Executioner never underestimated the terrible brutality of man. The human species had reason to be ashamed at the way it wantonly slaughtered its own kind. It was one of the reasons he existed. Why he waged his personal war against evil. In his own way he was trying to redress the balance. To even out the savagery of man. He sought out the transgressors and brought them to summary justice. His victories were small on the global scale, but without him the innocents would have no one to mark the pain of their suffering.

"Cooper, don't let me down. I want Frank back alive."

Bolan raised his mug. "Make me another coffee and we have a deal."

Lesley smiled briefly, pushing to her feet, as the apartment door crashed open under the impact of a heavy kick.

11

Three men burst into the apartment. Two held auto pistols. One covered Bolan. The other pushed the door shut. The third crossed the room and confronted Lesley.

"That's the bitch, Jardine," one of the men covering Bolan said.

Jardine grinned. He reached out to squeeze Lesley's shoulder, letting his hand slide in the direction of her breast.

"Hey," Bolan said.

"Make it an easy ride for the lady and shut your mouth," Jardine said. "We don't want any fuss."

"That so?" Bolan asked quietly.

"Yeah." Another easy grin. "And this could be interesting," he said, deliberately eyeing Lesley's figure.

"In your dreams," she said and threw the contents of her mug into his face.

The coffee was still hot enough to sting. Jardine gasped, raising a hand to wipe the coffee from his face. He recovered quickly, muttering an obscenity, then before Lesley could anticipate what was happening he backhanded her across the side of the face. The hard blow stunned her. She stumbled and went down on her knees, head hanging.

The gun trained on Bolan wavered briefly as its owner glanced across at Jardine. Bolan took the opportunity. His right hand swung up and around. He was still holding his own mug. He slammed it against the side of the gunman's face, the impact hard enough to open a gash over the guy's cheekbone. Bolan's left hand moved swiftly, his fingers clamping around the wrist of the hand holding the auto pistol. The Executioner took a quick step in close, locking the gun arm against his side. His big right hand closed over the pistol, finger sliding over the guy's trigger finger. Bolan yanked hard, bringing the muzzle around, lining up on Jardine. He didn't hesitate. The pistol cracked once, the 9 mm slug striking Jardine in the side of the neck. It passed through and exited on the far side in a bloody spatter.

The gunman, seeing the demise of his partner, concentrated his effort to break free. Bolan slammed his right elbow up into the guy's face, hearing a bone snap. The guy howled as his crushed nose spurted blood. Bolan used his elbow again. This time an equally savage blow that struck the target's throat and reduced tissue and cartilage to mush. As the choking, dying man fell back Bolan snatched the pistol from his fingers, dropped to a crouch and swiveled at the hip, the muzzle tracking in on the third guy, who was swinging his own pistol down in Bolan's direction.

Bolan fired first, his shot hitting the gunman in the chest, knocking him off balance and giving Bolan an almost leisurely time to make his next shot. That was into the heart, laying the guy facedown on the floor, his weapon spinning from his hand.

It was over in seconds. Efficient and brutal. Nothing fancy. No elaborate martial arts posturing or unnecessary noises.

It was not graceful combat.

It was killing.

Bolan was not proud of it. He had done what needed doing and that was it.

He crossed to Lesley. She was trembling. White-faced. Her gaze was on the man at her feet. Jardine's blood was pooling out across the polished wood of her living room floor.

His awkward movements slowing until there were no more. Bolan drew her to him and moved her away from death, easing her into the bedroom on the other side of the apartment. He felt her press her face against his shoulder. He held her until she had regained control.

"These are the men who want to find Frank," he said.

"Now I understand," she said. "They won't give up, will they?"

"The ones behind all this are desperate to get their hands on the information Frank found. So, no, they won't give up." He brushed his hand across her bruised cheek. "Neither will we. Okay?"

She drew breath, her face pale, uncertainty in her eyes. "I'll tell you where to find him."

As Bolan led her out of the room, on their way to the street and his waiting SUV, she said, "I really don't think I'd like this man Hoekken. Frank said he's the main security guy."

"You and me both," Bolan said, but he was thinking that sooner or later he was going to come face-to-face with the OTG head of security. It wasn't going to be a pleasant visit. Or a long one.

They reached street level. Bolan guided Lesley into the SUV. He started the engine and drove away from the apartment building. He used his cell phone to contact Barbara Price at the Farm. When she came on he laid out his needs.

"She goes into complete isolation," he said. "No informing anyone. All agencies, civil or federal. Too many hostile ears out there. Just keep her safe until you get the word from me. No one else. Understand?"

"Okay, Striker, I think I received the message."

Bolan sensed the thin veneer of tension in her tone.

"Hey, sorry. It's been a little rough out here. You didn't deserve that."

Price gave a soft chuckle. "Don't sweat it, tough guy. I

know what you're up against. Don't worry about the lady. She will get the best Stony Man treatment. Five star all the way. The team is on standby. Tell me where and when and they'll be en route."

"Take good care of her. She's a nice woman. She doesn't deserve what's happened. I'll be in touch."

Bud Casper had provided covert air transport for the Executioner on a couple of previous missions when Jack Grimaldi had been unavailable. The Stony Man pilot was just that today, working a mission with Able Team. Bolan had no qualms about asking for Casper's assistance. The flier, a veteran of the Gulf War, was an expert pilot with a taste for action. During his first encounter with Bolan he had almost died, as he'd been wounded and lost in the snows of Colorado's mountains. That experience had not deterred him from responding when Bolan called.

"Hey, Striker, been a while. I guess you'll be needing a ride somewhere?"

"Across the border. How's your Spanish? You ever heard of Puerto Laredo?"

"No, but I have a feeling I'm going to learn all about it."

"You still operating out of the same strip?"

"Oh, yes."

"It'll take me about three hours to reach you. Can you be ready to go?" Bolan asked.

"Point me in the direction and we'll be on our way."

"Bud, I'm not heading for a stroll in the park."

"Hell, Striker, I'd be ashamed to know you if that was the case."

BOLAN PUT IN A CALL to Stony Man for an update.

"Lesley Cornwell is on her way to a safe location with a

couple of our people," Brognola told him. "She'll be fine, Striker."

"That's all I needed to know."

"Here's something you might not want to hear. Word came back via the Billings, Montana, PD. Veronica Carella was discovered dead in her apartment. Police were called in to check after she failed to show up for work. No way to wrap this up nice, Striker. Signs are she was tortured before being shot."

"Par for the course," Bolan said. "Ordstrom's crew only have one rule they follow. If it stands in their way they just wipe it out. That's fine with me, Hal. We'll see how they like those rules applied to them. I'm sorry we didn't reach Carella's sister in time."

"As good as your intentions are, you can't save everyone."

"Won't be much consolation to Frank Carella." Bolan took a heartbeat's pause. "Has Bear come up with any more background on Ordstrom?"

"Have you got a couple of hours to spare? Cut to the bone, Ordstrom is a damn scary guy. His list of friends, backers and contacts could fill a telephone book. By the way, one of those friends *was* Colonel Bosley. Being who he is, our cyber wizard has been digging deep. Ordstrom has government and military contracts coming out of his ears and every other bodily orifice. He subcontracts and deals across the board. From what Bear has put together Ordstrom has even supplied covert weapons consignments for the CIA for their destabilizing operations in Latin America and the Middle East. Bottom line has him as a smart operator who doesn't mind getting his hands dirty as long as the payoff is large enough. He has high-level security, as well. Striker, this guy is as fireproof as they can get."

"Things change, Hal."

Brognola didn't need any expansion of that short response. He knew exactly what Bolan meant.

The Executioner was on line. He was tracking Ordstrom and his organization. He was like a locked-on missile, seeking its target with red-hot intensity. Once Bolan was locked in, he refused to let go.

"Keep us primed," Brognola said. "Hey, if Ordstrom's people got information out of Carella's sister they could be waiting in Puerto Laredo when you show up."

"I'm banking on it," the Executioner said.

IT WAS DARK WHEN Bolan drove in through the gates of the small airstrip, parking outside the hangar and hut that were the base of operations for Casper Air Services. Bud Casper was in the neat office setup, poring over the computer on his desk. He swung his chair around as Bolan stepped inside, pushing to his full height and thrusting out a hand.

"You made good time, Striker."

Bolan had a heavy bag with him. He placed it on the floor as he returned Casper's handshake.

"Time is something we're short of, Bud."

Casper grinned. "Subtle as ever. Don't worry, we're ready to go."

He led the way out of the office, securing the door, and headed across the concrete apron in the direction of a blue-and-white Beechcraft King Air 100. The twin turboprop aircraft had Casper's logo painted on the side of the fuselage.

"Nice," Bolan commented.

"Last one I had got totaled on a charter to Colorado," Casper said wryly. "Loved that Cessna."

He was referring to the first time Bolan had used him, the plane having to be abandoned in the heart of a heavy snowstorm. Stony Man had bankrolled the replacement aircraft and added Casper to the Farm's roster of people to be called on in times of emergency. Bud Casper had jumped at the chance of becoming a standby pilot. He knew just enough about the

Executioner's role and the Farm's covert background to refrain from asking questions. What he did know kept him curious *and* receptive.

The interior passenger cabin was fitted with custom leather seats and pale wood trim. Casper moved ahead to the flight deck as Bolan stowed his bag and sank into one of the seats.

"You mind if I crash?"

"Make yourself at home." Casper grinned. "Course is all logged in. We'll need a couple of stops to top up on fuel. Fly time around eight hours, depending on weather."

Bolan settled himself in the comfort of the deep cushioned seat. He heard the engines turning over, felt the aircraft start to move. By the time the plane left the ground Bolan was asleep.

The onboard navigation system had put the aircraft on course. Casper stayed at the controls for the first hour, checking and rechecking until he was satisfied, then set the autopilot and stepped back into the main cabin. He positioned one of the drop-down tables across two of the seats and produced a large flask he'd brought along. He poured hot coffee into mugs and sat back, waiting. The aroma of the rich coffee roused Bolan. He sat up, glancing across at Casper.

"Okay, I'll have some," he said.

Casper passed across the second mug.

"What's the deal, Striker?" he asked.

Casper had not asked for details when Bolan had invited him to join the mission. Now he wanted to find out what he had bought himself into, and Bolan told him. He kept the briefing as concise as he could without omitting any of the necessary details. Casper listened without interruption until Bolan completed his update.

"So Carella is hiding out in Puerto Laredo. The guy doesn't trust anyone. He realizes Ordstrom has a long reach and contacts that could easily include law enforcement. He's sitting on information Ordstrom and his crew need to get their hands on so it can be destroyed. If those files are made public OTG goes to the wall and so will all the people wrapped up in this mess."

"These sons of bitches need stopping. Bad enough our guys being hurt in combat. Having to face it with crap equipment…" Casper broke off, unable to finish the sentence. "Doesn't this bastard Ordstrom already make enough money?"

"He's in so deep now he most likely can't remember how it all started. Ordstrom is in bed with so many partners he can't even walk away."

"Then we'll just have to show him the way, Striker."

13

Casper had checked out the local area around Puerto Laredo.
He had located a small airstrip some ten miles to the east of
the town. It was barely dawn when the plane touched down,
Casper throttling back and bringing the aircraft to a smooth
stop alongside the couple of old hangars and the wooden
building that served as the control office. He cut the power
and climbed out, stretching his legs as he crossed to speak
with the guy on duty. Bolan learned then that the flier spoke
fluent Spanish and was negotiating a deal with the Mexican.

"This is Señor Deaga Soterro. He doesn't speak English.
This place is owned by his family. He tells me that business
has been slow lately so he can rent us one of the hangars to hide
the plane. And he has a couple of cars out back so we can hire
one to take us to Puerto Laredo. He says there are a couple of
good hotels in town. One is owned by his wife's uncle. He will
call ahead for us. I explained we were looking for someone.
An old friend. He says his wife's uncle may be able to help."

"Having you along, Bud, might be useful after all,"
Bolan said, then turned to the Mexican and spoke to him
in his own language.

"Have there been any other Americans through here
recently?" Bolan asked.

Soterro shook his head. "No. You are the first for many
weeks. I have regular customers who fly down for the deep-
water fishing off Puerto Laredo, but that season is not for some

time yet. Ask at the hotel. Pascal will know if strangers have been around."

"Thank you for your assistance," Bolan said as he paid the man the agreed amount of cash Casper had negotiated, adding a few hundred extra dollars. "Will you make sure the plane is fully fuelled for our return?"

Soterro nodded. "Of course." He looked long and hard at Bolan, studying the American's eyes. "Take care, *señor. Vaya con Dios.*"

As they headed in the direction of the vehicle they had hired Casper said, "Striker, you never told me you spoke the lingo."

"Bud, you never asked." Bolan stopped beside the vehicle. "Nothing in the contract says you have to get involved any further. This could get messy."

"If you think I'm sitting on my butt out here, Striker, it isn't going to happen. I'm in all the way, buddy, so save your breath."

AN HOUR LATER, with the day brightening around them, they were on the narrow strip of road that led to Puerto Laredo. The car they had rented from the Mexican was a Dodge 4x4 around ten years old. It had been well maintained and the motor ran smoothly.

"Did Carella's lady friend actually pin down where he might be hiding out?" Casper asked.

"She told me they sometimes stayed in a small house about three miles the other side of Puerto Laredo. Near the beach. But there was also a larger place they used in the hills over-looking town."

"Or he might have gone native and just decided to camp out in the brush."

"Another possibility."

Puerto Laredo had most likely not changed its outward ap-pearance in the last century. The architecture was classic Mexican, the atmosphere laid-back and the people presented a friendly face. The wide town plaza opened on the curve of the deep-water bay that provided Puerto Laredo with its harbor. A half-dozen ancient fishing boats were tied up at the quayside. Even at this early hour the plaza was busy. As Bolan guided the Dodge across the plaza he spotted the hotel Soterro had told them to visit. Bolan parked just beyond.

"Stay here and…"

"Keep my eyes open," Casper said.

Bolan crossed to the entrance and went inside the hotel. The surprisingly large lobby had a decorated tile floor and a carved reception desk that would not have looked out of place in any high-class hotel. Large fans, suspended from the ceiling, stirred the air. To the right of the lobby an arched doorway, which led into the bar. At the desk a young Mexican woman raised her eyes as Bolan approached. She smiled at him.

"How may I help you, *señor?*" she asked in perfect English. Her voice was soft, with a gentle accent, the words slipping easily over her plump, soft lips.

"I see you were expecting me, *señorita*. Then you will know I wish to speak to Señor Pascal."

"He will be right with you."

Bolan watched her walk toward the door behind the desk, appreciating the gentle sway of curving hips beneath the slim skirt, her long black hair shimmering. The woman stepped through the door and Bolan heard the murmur of conversation. The woman returned and beckoned for Bolan to step behind the desk and enter the office. As he walked by her he caught the tantalizing scent of her perfume, saw the slight movement as she parted her lips in the moment before she turned and left.

The office was cluttered and dominated by a huge, ornate wooden desk. Bolan noticed the modern laptop sitting in the middle of the chaos. Behind the desk a lean, dark man, dressed in immaculate whites, stood and extended a slim hand. Bolan judged him to be in his early sixties. Handsome, perfectly groomed, his eyes bright and alert.

"Señor Pascal, I am grateful for your time."

Pascal nodded. "It is my pleasure. Please sit down." Bolan took one of the seats facing the desk. "May I offer you something? A drink? Something to smoke, perhaps?"

"*Gracias,* no."

"Deaga told me you are seeking a friend who may be here in Puerto Laredo?"

"Yes."

"He also said you were interested in whether other Americanos have visited Puerto Laredo recently?"

"That's right."

"It occurs to me, *señor*…?"

"Cooper."

"*Señor* Cooper, it occurs to me that your visit here is not entirely, how shall I say, for recreation. Is your friend in trouble?"

Bolan smiled. The man was no fool. Nor was he under any illusions about Bolan's presence in Puerto Laredo.

"He could be in a great deal of trouble if I don't locate him first," Bolan said.

"Is that why you carry a gun?" Pascal was staring at the barely noticeable bulge under Bolan's jacket. "Are you a police official?"

"A loose term, *Señor* Pascal."

"I see. This *friend?* Is he a criminal?"

"No. The man is hiding because he possess information that would expose criminal acts and the people involved in a conspiracy."

"The other men you have asked about? They are seeking him, too?"

"If they find him they'll kill him. As they have already killed others trying to find how to get to him."

"So why did this man come to Puerto Laredo?"

"He's been here before. It's a place he thought no one knew he'd visited. A safe place."

"Would I know him?"

"Perhaps. His name is Frank Carella."

Pascal spread his hands. "*Señor* Carella? Yes, I know him. He has been here a number of times. With the beautiful *Señorita* Cornwell." He leaned forward, his face grave with concern. "Please do not tell me she has been hurt."

"She's safe. In protective custody after an attempt on her life."

"*Gracias a Dios.* Tell me what I may do to help."

"Directions to the places Carella used when he came here."

"That is easy."

Pascal reached for a pen and paper. He sketched details of the routes to the spots where Carella and Lesley Cornwell had stayed during past visits.

"The first one is no more than three miles on the other side of town. It overlooks the beach. The second, maybe ten, twelve miles inland. In the hills to the east. Very, what is the word you say, yes, isolated."

Pascal's directions confirmed what Lesley Cornwell had told Bolan. "You haven't seen Carella?"

"No. This is the first I have heard of his visit."

"He wouldn't want to broadcast it. As far as you know there have been no others asking questions?"

Pascal shook his head. "To my knowledge, no."

"Are there any police in town?"

"Only a two man force," Pascal said. "Puerto Laredo is only a small town. Nothing of consequence happens here. If anything serious takes place Ortega, the chief of police, can send for help from La Paz. Tell me, *Señor* Cooper, are you expecting problems?"

"Expectation keeps me on my toes."

"*Muy buena.*"

"Does Carella have a vehicle here?" Bolan asked.

"Each time he comes he hires a car from Ramos." Pascal saw the question in Bolan's eyes and reached for the telephone. When his call was answered he spoke in rapid Spanish that Bolan found hard to follow.

"*Señor* Carella rented a car from Ramos a few days ago. It is a light blue American Cadillac." Pascal smiled. "Not the best car for driving up into those hills, but it was the only decent one Ramos had available. Like Ramos the car is old, but dependable. And before you ask, Ramos told me some Mexicans, not from Puerto Laredo, have been asking questions about a lone American. They were going from business to business, especially the *cantinas*. I am afraid someone, somewhere, may have seen *Señor* Carella."

"I expected that might happen. It means they might know what vehicle to look out for." Bolan showed the Mexican his cell phone. "Will I get a signal in the hills?"

Pascal spread his hands in the universal gesture.

"*Quién sabe?* It will depend where you are." He took back the paper he had sketched directions on and added a telephone number. "This will find me, *señor.*"

"Thank you. I have to go now. Time is not on our side today."

Pascal watched the tall American walk out of the hotel. He wondered if he would see him again. And he wondered, sadly, whether Frank Carella was alive or already dead.

14

As they drove through town, finding the coast road that wound a torturous way through the lush terrain, both Bolan and Casper kept their eyes open. The fact that Arnold Hoekken and his full team didn't appear to have shown up in Puerto Laredo did little to satisfy Bolan. He preferred to go with his instincts. And those inner voices were telling him to stay alert. Hoekken would have made sure he had people on the ground well before he and his main crew showed up, even if it meant hiring local talent. If he read the man right Hoekken would make La Paz his main base, moving on to Puerto Laredo from there once he had assembled his equipment and crew. He could easily have hired a forward team from the city and sent them on ahead. If the men were Mexican they would have been able to merge into the local populace without arousing much suspicion.

Bolan would have been the first to accept he was only making an educated guess. It wasn't the first time and would not be the last. Part of combat was stepping into the shoes of the enemy and figuring his upcoming moves. It was a means of equipping himself with the foresight to be one step ahead. If it worked it gained him the advantage. Even if it failed there was always the element of at least being geared up to expect something surprising, and even that could have a positive outcome.

Beside him Bud Casper rode in silence, only his eyes moving as he checked their surroundings.

"Bud, you not so sure staying with me was such a good idea?"

Casper glanced at Bolan. "Weird thing to say."

"You've been quiet for a while is all."

"Been doing some thinking about this whole Ordstrom thing. I know I said earlier how I felt. I can't figure how our boys could get sold down the river so easy. Hell, they're out there, walking the line every day because they were sent by the government. No damn way they deserve a deal like this."

"No arguments from me, Bud. The way I see it Ordstrom and his partners have tied all this up between them. Military contracts mean big money. Shaving money off safety levels by producing substandard equipment adds to the profits. Backdoor deals with unfriendly regimes mean even more. When so many people become drawn into the deals it means self-protection is paramount. So they buy that. Wherever it's needed. The military. Government cover-ups. Law enforcement. Hike the price and people can be persuaded to look the other way. Bad as it sounds, these things happen. We live in a world of opportunity and even if the bottom line means putting people in danger, others will hold out their hand and take the big bucks. Money, personal advancement, hunger for power. They all have one thing in common—they feed on man's frailties."

"It doesn't make it justifiable."

"No, it doesn't."

Bolan eased off the gas as he spotted the marker indicating the turn that, hopefully, would take them to the beach property Carella had used before. Rolling the Dodge off the dirt trail, Bolan stopped. He cut the motor.

"We walk in from here," he said, easing the Beretta from its holster.

Casper, his own Glock automatic in his hand, joined Bolan at the front of the Dodge. "Want me to circle around and come in from the beach side?"

"Okay. Bud, careful. These guys are not playing games."

"Middle name is caution."

They parted company, each moving into and through the greenery that dominated the tropical environment.

It took a good five minutes before Bolan made out the low roof of the house. Beyond it he could see the white strip of beach and the blue water of the gulf.

With his objective in sight, the Executioner took time to check out the house and the immediate area around it. No vehicles in sight. Not conclusive no one was there. The soft lapping of waves against the shore was the only sound after the local birdsong. Bolan saw no movement. None *outside* the house.

He moved in closer and crouched against the rear wall, pausing before he continued along the base of the building, easing forward to check beyond the corner.

He froze at the image of a muscular man lounging at the end of the timber porch fronting the house. The man was armed. A pump-action shotgun was cradled in his thick arms. His thick black hair and dark complexion marked him as a local. Local as in La Paz, Bolan figured.

As Bolan eyeballed him, the guy turned and began to speak to someone out of Bolan's sight. The words were in Spanish and Bolan had to listen hard to translate.

"How much longer we gonna have to stay here?"

"Until the man says different."

"Watching over an empty house?"

"Maybe the American will still show. And if he doesn't we still get paid for lazing around in the sun. Think of that, Chico. Money to spend when we get back to the city."

"I can't wait," Chico replied. "I hate the country. It stinks and it's full of peasants."

Chico turned and spat over the porch rail. Lips pursed, he looked directly at Bolan. For a split second he was motionless, then he shouted at his unseen partner, dragging the muzzle of his shotgun in Bolan's direction.

Bolan reacted instantly, digging in his feet and launching

himself away from the side of the house. As he tucked and rolled he heard the shotgun boom and felt the tug of shot against the leg of his pants. Then he was down, swiveling and coming up on one knee, his Beretta tracking, finger easing back on the trigger to release a tri-burst that hit the Mexican in the chest. Chico gasped, stumbling back away from the rail. The shotgun boomed a second time, the shot blasting into the porch floor at Chico's feet as he started to go down.

On his feet Bolan moved toward the house. He saw Chico's partner rushing to step down off the porch. The man carried an identical weapon—a powerful shotgun. He hit the top step, then turned his head at something that caught his eye.

It was Bud Casper, angling in to meet the Mexican, his handgun up and ready. The Mexican racked his shotgun, pulled the barrel around. Casper fired two hard, close shots. The Mexican hardman went down without a sound, on his back, staring up at the sun.

15

The Executioner checked the bodies. The men carried little of value as far as Bolan was concerned. Some cash, cigarettes, lighters. No ID. No cell phones.

"Not exactly mines of information," Casper said.

Bolan went into the house. It obviously had not been occupied for some time. With Casper on his heels he returned to their vehicle. He drove back to the road, consulted the map Pascal had drawn and swung the Dodge around.

"The hillside retreat?" Casper asked.

Bolan simply nodded. He was calculating the odds of reaching Carella before Hoekken's crew. Finding men waiting at the beach house suggested Hoekken's people were already in motion. And if Carella had not been at the first location, would the opposition strike lucky and find him at the other house? The answer was one Bolan didn't even want to consider. But he had to play the cards that had been dealt.

He pushed the Dodge as hard as he could. Fortunately the roads around Puerto Laredo were quiet, with little traffic. Bolan passed everything he saw without easing off the gas. Casper decided his companion must have broken every speed violation on the books, but kept his thoughts to himself.

The side road marked on the map came up. Pascal had even noted the sign that indicated the turn. Bolan took it at speed, feeling the Dodge's suspension take the strain. He kept his foot down hard, the vehicle bouncing and rattling as it sped along the rutted, dusty road.

"About five miles in," Casper observed. "Speed you're going, Striker, we should do it in a couple of minutes."

Bolan managed a grin at Casper's remark. He maintained his pace for at least three of those five miles, only easing off as they got closer to the isolated house. He slowed and pulled the Dodge off the track, reversing in beneath the overhanging branches of the trees edging the road. Thick undergrowth gave way as the Dodge pushed deep. Bolan cut the motor.

"End of the line, Bud. We hike the rest of the way."

Bolan checked his handguns, Beretta and Desert Eagle, making sure he had extra magazines for both in the pouches clipped to his belt. He scanned the way ahead, checking the swathes of trees and heavy foliage, green and lush.

"Nice piece of country," Casper said, returning his own reloaded auto pistol to the holster on his hip.

"Let's go walk some of it," Bolan said.

The sun was well into its swing across the sky. Apart from the soft sound of their footsteps the hills were quiet. The forested slopes spread out around them, continuing up to the crests of the range of hills. Turning to look back Bolan saw the hazy blue of the ocean far below. Somewhere down there was Puerto Laredo.

They moved on, walking parallel to the narrow road, using the undergrowth as cover. When the road made a sharp left bend Bolan raised a hand to warn Casper. A couple of hundred feet ahead, slightly down slope, was their destination.

The house was midsized, with a number of outbuildings scattered around it. Beyond the house the land still showed faint indications where fields had been marked out. The place had the appearance of a hill farm, long deserted. The pale blue Cadillac, parked near the house, looked out of place in the idyllic setting. So did the two black 4x4s. They were equipped with roof-mounted spotlights, high suspension and wide, heavy-tread tires.

Crouching beside Bolan, Casper sighed.

"Hope we ain't late, Striker."

"Let's not make it any later," Bolan said.

They broke cover and began the slow advance that would bring them in at the rear of the house. There were no signs of movement, suggesting any visitors must be inside the building. Bolan hoped it stayed that way until they reached the house.

It wasn't the first time wishful thinking turned on its heel and changed course. Bolan's desire for a quiet insertion into the enemy camp was destined to go belly-up. With Casper close by Bolan closed on the main house, moving by an open-fronted structure that had once been a smoke house. Now fallen into disrepair, with sagging poles and gaps in the roof, the building looked empty. As Bolan passed the structure he sensed something out of kilter—a suspicion that he and Casper were not alone. He continued on his forward track, letting his feelings grow, eyes turning to check the deep shadows just inside the building.

He caught a fragment, a sliver of movement. One deep block of shadow was disturbed by additional sensations of motion.

It was enough for the Executioner.

He never questioned his natural responses to bad feelings. He simply reacted. Bolan reached back, grabbing a handful of Casper's shirt and yanking the pilot to one side.

Casper shouted.

There was a rattle followed by the hard sound of a shotgun. The blast cleaved the air where Casper had been seconds before. As he tugged Casper out of the potential line of fire, Bolan's right hand was fielding the big Desert Eagle.

The shooter exposed himself as he stepped forward for a second shot, angling the barrel of the pump-action shotgun as he prepared to fire again.

The .44 Magnum pistol in Bolan's hand hammered out its first shot, the big slug powering out to tear its way through the shooter's throat, shearing away flesh and underlying muscle. Blood washed out of the gaping, ragged wound and the shooter flew back, his weapon dropping to the ground.

Casper had tumbled hard, sliding across the dusty ground. Hearing the shots he realized what had happened and tugged his own handgun free even as he was scrambling to his feet. As he rose he caught a glimpse of another hostile figure emerging from cover, the guy cutting loose with a battered, but plainly functional, AK-47. The harsh crack of the Russian assault rifle, fired on the move, galvanized Casper into a response. He raised his Glock in a two-handed grip, tracking his target and firing a trio of close shots that put his target down hard and fast.

Beside him Bolan was engaging a second shooter. The guy had seen his two partners taken out in the space of seconds and he was unsure which of his targets to go for. That pause cost him dearly as Bolan lined up his combat pistol and hit him with two more rounds. The guy was whipped off his feet, slamming facedown on the hard ground, a pair of bloody exit holes in his back.

Okay, Bolan decided, soft probe gone.

Enemy figures unknown. Time to assess that later. A strategic retreat was called for.

Bolan gestured to Casper and the pair turned away from the house, angling in the direction of the surrounding trees. They had covered over half the distance when the clatter of automatic gunfire sounded behind them and lines of slugs clawed and chewed at the hard earth around them. The solid whack of the slugs kicked up chunks of soil, then stripped bark from the trees as Bolan and Casper hit the tree line. Even with the cover around them they kept moving until they had created a distance in amongst the greenery.

As Bolan called a halt sounds of pursuit could be heard. Leaning around the thick trunk of a covering tree Bolan picked out the moving figures closing on the tree line and decided they needed reminding that their quarry wasn't about to quit.

Bolan raised the Desert Eagle and sighted down on one of the aggressors, the man seeming to be in charge as he continually yelled orders at the other gunmen. He led the target until he was sure of his shot, then put a single slug into the guy's skull. The impact took away a chunk of fleshy bone and brain.

The sight of their crew boss dropping to the ground made the surviving shooters back away as they argued between themselves in voluble Spanish. Bolan decided it would only be a temporary reprieve before they attacked again. In that time he and Casper needed to gain ground. Bolan turned and waved his partner forward. They cut through the stand, moving in a wide circle. The tree cover was not going to protect them for long, Bolan realized, and once they emerged they would be targets again.

Ahead he saw the trees thinning out. Bolan waved Casper to cut around in a move that would bring him to the rear of the opposition's parked vehicles. He maintained his forward track.

He also saw the two armed men flanking the vehicles. One was busy talking into a handheld com unit, already waving his arm to warn his partner.

Out of the corner of his eye Bolan spotted Casper on the far side of the parked 4x4s. The pilot had assessed the situation and had picked his target.

Bolan heard a shout behind him. He picked up the sound of someone crashing through the undergrowth. The shooters were coming in faster than he'd expected. He stayed on course, the Magnum tracking on the guy with the com set. He was close enough for a shot.

He took it.

He saw the guy jerk backward as the brutal impact of the

.44 Magnum slug ripped into his chest. The guy bounced off the side of the truck, the weapon in his hands spilling free as he went down. Before the guy hit the ground the double crack of Casper's Glock reached Bolan as he took down his own target.

With the seconds ticking away Bolan ran forward, holstered the Magnum and snatched up the dropped submachine gun. It was a battered Uzi 9 mm. He turned as he straightened, fingers sliding across the weapon, making sure it was cocked. He caught the pursuing crew as they began to filter from the trees, the stuttering crackle of the Uzi loud in the still air. His measured burst caught the killing crew, slugs hammering into flesh and chipping tree bark. They stumbled, bleeding, screaming, and crashed to ground that became dappled with their blood.

The Uzi locked empty with a metallic click. Brass casings littered the ground at Bolan's feet. He ejected the empty magazine, bending over the weapon's previous owner to snatch extra magazines from the harness the guy wore. As the Executioner inserted a fresh load and snapped back the cocking lever he heard one of the 4x4 engines fire up.

Casper was behind the wheel, waiting. Bolan swung into the passenger seat and the vehicle moved off. Rounding the far edge of the trees they saw the second truck running parallel with them. As Casper drove by, Bolan rolled down the window, leaning out to fire short bursts into front and rear tires, shredding the rubber. The pursuing 4x4 slewed off track as the tires disintegrated, the vehicle now running on its rims. It fell behind and armed figures jumped from the cab, opening fire. Slugs hammered the rear of Bolan's vehicle. The tailgate window shattered.

"We still don't know if Carella was inside the house," Casper said.

Bolan checked the magazine. Enough for a short burst. "Only way to find out is by going back," he said.

"My own fault for asking."

Casper hauled on the steering wheel, turning the 4x4 in the tightest circle he could manage. Then he gunned the motor and sent the heavy vehicle at a dead run toward the crew grouped around the stalled vehicle. "I just hope you know what you're doing," he said.

The three surviving Mexicans saw the 4x4 speeding at them. The abrupt reversal of tactics had them staring for a few seconds, then their weapons rose and they opened fire. The hesitation was their final mistake.

The front of the hurtling 4x4 struck one man head-on. His screaming form flipped up and over the hood. He crashed against the windshield, leaving a greasy swathe of bloody matter on the glass, then slid up the windshield, across the roof and slammed to the ground just behind the 4x4.

Bolan leaned out the passenger side window and triggered his last shots at the remaining pair of shooters. One guy flopped loosely to the ground, the survivor spun away with a burst and bloody shoulder.

"Bring her around," Bolan said.

As Casper spun the 4x4 Bolan discarded the Uzi and grabbed his Beretta 93-R. He was out of the 4x4 before it slithered to a stop, his long legs carrying him across to where the wounded Mexican was trying to bring his weapon on line one-handed. Bolan launched a powerful kick that knocked the weapon from the gunman's hand. It spun away to a safe distance, allowing Bolan to bend over and drag the moaning Mexican to his feet.

"Looks like you're the lucky one," Bolan said. "You get to give the answers I need."

The man stared at Bolan, shaking his head. He claimed he didn't understand English.

Bolan's expression showed no trace of humor. "Then it is lucky again that I speak your language," he said in Spanish.

"I will tell you nothing," the man responded.

"Your choice, *hombre*." Bolan glanced at the man's shoulder. His shots had blown out a chunk of flesh and muscle, splintering the bone, leaving jagged shards protruding from the ragged, bloody flesh. The messy wound was bleeding heavily. "If you don't get that wound seen to it's all going to be over for you."

The Mexican attempted to appear indifferent, but his sidelong glance at the mangled shoulder suggested he was running out of macho bravado.

"Just tell me where Frank Carella is. Do that and I promise to help you."

Casper had gone across to check out the house. When he came back he caught Bolan's eye, shaking his head. "He's not there. Looks like he has been but the place is empty."

"Back to you, friend," Bolan said. "Help yourself."

"No one else can," Casper added.

"Tell me, or stay here and bleed to death."

"Either way I will most probably die. The man who hired us in La Paz said if we fail he would kill us himself."

"Is he here in Puerto Laredo?" Bolan asked.

"No. He waits for the rest of his people. Then they will come."

"Carella?" Bolan asked.

"He was not here. He had been at the house. We found tracks that showed he has gone farther up into the hills. Some went after him. We were waiting here in case he doubled back."

"Did you know about us?"

"The man Hoekken warned us that a Yankee was also searching for Carella. If you showed up we were told to kill you."

"Still making friends then, Striker," Casper said.

Bolan glanced at him. "It's a talent."

They moved aside.

"You believe him?" Casper asked.

"Evidence says he's telling the truth."

"We going after him?"

"I am. You take our *compadre* back to town and get him medical help. Check out the local situation."

Casper wasn't all that keen, but he made no fuss. He understood there was no compromise with the Executioner. The man was a deadly enemy but he had within him compassion that allowed him to exhibit another side to his character. Casper couldn't fault that.

16

Bolan felt the loose surface of the rough track beneath the tires, even the solid base of the 4x4 struggling to maintain an even run. He held the wheel steady, muscles bunching to contain the rugged vehicle, despite the power steering. It was not made easy by the twisting route of the track, or the thick foliage that had spread on either side. The intertwining tops of trees often closed to the point where they created a near impenetrable canopy. One moment Bolan was in bright sunlight, the next plunged into dark gloom.

He was banking on Frank Carella staying close to the trail. The dense forested terrain on either side would bring any kind of travel down almost to a standstill and that would have been the last thing Carella needed. Putting himself in the man's position Bolan would have been determined to get himself well up-country. If Carella wanted to hide, this was as good a place as any.

Bolan stayed in his Carella mind-set. Trying to imagine how the man would act in such a situation. Taken as logical thinking, Carella's single-minded attempt to hide himself away in this remote area might not have been the wisest move. Carella had been hoping to escape the attention of his enemies by fleeing to the isolated Mexican location. That had already proved to be a delusion. Ordstrom's crew had still found him.

Bolan's theorizing went a step further. Even if isolation had worked Carella would have been no better off when it came to exposing OTG. Marooned in the Mexican backcountry, away from any influencing body, Carella's incriminating evidence meant nothing. Not only would he still be on his own, but there would also be no way of getting his information to anyone who mattered. Carella's escape would have simply backed him into a corner that offered no way out. It was a lose-lose situation. Bolan could not have made such a decision. Affirmative action was his creed. Gather your strength and take it to the enemy. The old adage still held true—when there were no more options, attack. Bolan made no personal criticism concerning Carella's decisions. Each man played according to his own beliefs, the driving force that defined each individual. Carella's actions did not mark him as a lesser man. His way of life differed from Mack Bolan's by an eternity. But it was worth as much. Carella followed the rules of civilized society, but when he had tried to do what was right the enormity of the opposition had pushed him to his limit. Realizing he could not fight Ordstrom and live, Frank Carella had backed away, hoping to give himself space and time to consider his options. Now Bolan was going to give him the chance to engage those options.

The terrain leveled out, the dense foliage and trees thinning to allow Bolan to see his way a little clearer. He was still driving into hostile territory, knowing that Hoekken's crew was in the vicinity and he was bound to make contact with them soon.

The not-too-distant crackle of auto fire warned Bolan the moment was closer than he might have imagined. He locked in on the sound, swung the 4x4 around and hoped his intervention did not prove to be too late.

17

Ahead of Bolan a lone figure, backpack bouncing from his shoulders, was running to get away from a group of armed men. Bolan didn't need an introduction to verify he had found Frank Carella.

Bolan pulled the Desert Eagle. He needed the weapon's extra punch here. The situation called for hard, killing shots, allowing for the distance, and the big .44 Magnum would provide that.

As he hit the ground running, turning to face the first of Hoekken's wipeout crew, Bolan's hand swung the Desert Eagle's muzzle on track. He squeezed the trigger and saw the target stagger back as the heavy slug hit dead center in the chest. The guy fired off a burst in reflex, his weapon already pointing skyward. Bolan had moved on, catching up with the second shooter. The ponytailed guy triggered a burst in Carella's direction that plowed up chunks of Mexican real estate. The Desert Eagle boomed, spewing flame, and the slug caught the shooter behind his left ear, tearing out a hefty chunk of lower skull and half his jaw on the way out. The screaming man fell in a bone-crunching sprawl, giving up his weapon as he clutched at his ruined flesh.

Bolan saw Carella reach the cover of timber, gaining a little relief. It wouldn't last long, Bolan figured. There were still other shooters in the area. They would home in on the shooting. As he cut over in Carella's direction Bolan spotted another figure, armed, pushing out from thick foliage. The guy saw Bolan and reached for the submachine gun slung from his shoulder. Bolan turned, pistol in both hands, and centered on the guy before putting two shots into his upper body. The man fell back, tangling up in the thick foliage, and died there, half standing, his blood coursing down his heavy gut.

Powering up, Bolan reached the spot where Carella had entered the tree line. He caught sight of the man just ahead, pushing at the thick underbrush.

"Frank, I'm here to help. No time to discuss the how, just come with me and I'll get you out of this mess," he called out.

Bolan reached Carella as the American turned to face him. Carella's face was dirt-streaked, sweaty, his flesh scratched from the thick foliage. His eyes betrayed his emotional state as he stared at Bolan, at the big .44 Magnum pistol in his hand. He thrust out a grubby hand to ward off what he imagined was a continuing threat.

"Who the hell are you?"

"Matt Cooper. I'm here because Lesley told me where you were. Because Francis Nelson was a friend. Is that enough?"

"Just like that? You show up out here just like that?"

"Questions later. Let's go, Frank. You know what they've already done. Who they've killed. You want to stop it, come with me."

He grabbed Carella's shirt and hauled the man in the direction he wanted them to go. Bolan had picked up the heavy crackle of undergrowth being disturbed and knew pursuit was not far off. He half turned, picking out movement yards behind, the glint of sunlight on gunmetal. He raised the pistol and fired. Heard the ragged cry of pain as his shot found its target.

"Get moving. Let's go."

Carella's immobility vanished. He stumbled forward, Bolan close behind.

They ran, pushing through low-hanging branches and tangled undergrowth that snagged and pulled at their clothing.

Carella stumbled once, almost going down, but the too-close sound of gunfire ripping through the trees spurred him on. He hauled himself upright and kept his balance.

Bolan was counting off the distance to where he had left the 4x4. They needed to reach it before Hoekken's crew closed the gap and their shots became personal. He spotted the black shape of the vehicle twenty feet on their left and told Carella to turn in that direction.

"Black four-by-four. Once we clear the trees, head straight for it. Get in the back, down on the floor."

As they cleared the trees, the 4x4 looming, Carella did exactly what Bolan had instructed. He went for the rear door, yanking it open.

An armed figure rose from a crouch at the front of the 4x4, weapon already coming into play. His attention was focused on Carella, not Bolan, who was a few steps behind.

"Hey, *gringo,* you not going any farther," the man said.

Bolan, still moving, turned and hit the guy with a body slam that hammered him against the side of the vehicle. The shooter grunted. He was a hard-bodied guy, well-built, but Bolan's surprise strike caught him unprepared. Bolan caught a handful of thick black hair, yanked hard and slammed the guy's face against the thick metal of the 4x4's hood. The shooter gasped as his nose was crushed violently out of shape, bright blood spurting thickly. Before he could recover, Bolan jammed the muzzle of the Desert Eagle against his upper body and put two shots into him. The angled slugs blew through his ribs and body and exited via his spine in an ugly burst of red. As the man fell Bolan snatched the Uzi from his limp hands and reached for the driver's door. He dropped the submachine gun on the floor, jammed the Desert Eagle back into its holster and reached for the starter. The 4x4's powerful motor burst into life. Bolan hit the stick, freed the hand-brake and slammed his foot hard down on the gas pedal. Grass and dirt spewed up from beneath the spinning wheels and the big vehicle moved off, bouncing and sliding across the rough terrain as the wheels fought for traction.

Behind him Frank Carella was thrown about on the floor of the 4x4, his body battered against the base of the seats.

Bolan was aiming the 4x4 in the direction of the trail that had brought him here, aware that Hoekken's crew would not be lingering in their response. That was proven when he saw the dark shape of their own 4x4 coming into view, armed figures scrambling onboard even as it picked up speed. Windows were wound down so that armed men could lean out and open fire. The first bursts were short. The second round of shots, adjusted for range, were on target.

"Son of a bitch," Carella yelled, throwing himself back down on the floor of the truck as the hail of slugs pounded the vehicle.

Bolan hauled the wheel around, feeling the frame of the vehicle groan under the strain. The heavy 4x4 tail slid, bouncing as it hit the edge of the trail. Another burst of gunfire shattered a rear window, fragments of broken glass showering the interior.

"They trying to kill us, or what?" Carella asked in frustration.

"Yeah," Bolan said over his shoulder. "I thought you'd already figured that one out for yourself."

"Easy for you to say. Does this happen to you all the time?"

"There are quieter days."

Carella remained below window level, hugging the carpeted floor of the 4x4 again. It was not the most comfortable place to be with the vehicle speeding across uneven terrain, but he decided it was preferable to being shot. His world had been turned upside down from the moment he had walked out of the OTG facility with the two flash drives. Death and violence had become the order of the day. A living nightmare that refused to go away, and he accepted that if this man he knew as Cooper had not come into his life he would be dead.

Carella was scared, confused, well out of his depth, yet there was a stubborn refusal inside that would not allow him to quit. The relentless determination of OTG to keep him silent about what he had found had simply reinforced his desire to expose what they had done. That stubbornness was placing him directly in the firing line. Arnold Hoekken, backed up by his teams of hardmen, was set on wiping out Carella and regaining possession of the incriminating files. The security man's disregard of Carella's rights, his brutal pursuit, had added fuel to the fire. Carella was no killer. He was simply an ordinary man with a sense of right and wrong, and no amount of pressure, or threats, would make him stand meekly by while Hoekken threw his hostile force against Carella.

"Can't we do something to stop them?" Carella asked.

"I was just thinking the same thing myself," Bolan said.

He didn't explain what he was considering. There was no time for that. Bolan hit the brake, swinging the wheel, and brought the 4x4 around in a tight circle, dust billowing up in heavy clouds. As the vehicle came to a juddering halt Bolan snatched up the Uzi and booted open his door, dropping to the ground and rolling beneath the 4x4. He flat-crawled the length of the vehicle, the Uzi pushed in front. As he reached the level of the rear wheels Bolan heard the chase car come to a close stop. Despite the dust swirl he made out the shape of the vehicle. He saw doors swing open and witnessed the hurried emergence of the armed passengers. He didn't allow them the opportunity to organize themselves. The muzzle of the Uzi tracked, located its targets and then crackled harshly, shell cases littering the ground around him. He hit the opposition with full auto from the 32-round magazine, the concentrated 9 mm fire catching the opposition fully exposed. Two of the hardmen went down from the first burst. They sprawled on the ground, one clutching his punctured chest, the second kicked into a paralyzed curl, a low whine of sound coming from his lips.

The Executioner immediately slid himself around the rear wheel, tracking in with the Uzi to pick up on the last guy to exit the vehicle. He was on the far side, having seen his two partners go down and unsure where the gunfire had come from. When he moved—his first and last mistake—he was still seeking someone standing upright, so his gaze was not in Bolan's direction. The guy carried a heavy automatic pistol in one hand and it might as well have been cotton candy on a stick. The man carrying it had no idea where he needed to aim it and Mack Bolan had no intention of advancing that kind of information. As the lone hardman moved forward, his upper body showing above the flat expanse of the 4x4's hood, Bolan adjusted the angle of the Uzi's muzzle and swept his target with a sustained burst that ripped into the upper chest and then the throat. The guy made a garbled sound as he twisted on one foot, falling out of Bolan's sight. The sound of his body hitting the ground was heavy.

Bolan rolled out from beneath the 4x4, rising to a crouch as he scanned the area. He knew the pair of hardmen in front of him were dead. The third guy, out of sight behind the car, was still an unknown quantity and Bolan was taking no chances. He moved quickly, skirting the rear of the car and leaning out so he could check out the guy. Only when he saw the hunched body, facing upward, chest and throat ravaged by 9 mm fire, did he ease off. As Bolan stood upright he took a look through the windows. The vehicle was empty. He walked to the front of the car.

"You can come out, Frank," he called.

Bolan gathered up all the discarded weapons, adding the handguns he found on the dead men. They were placed in the 4x4, along with the extra loaded magazines. By the time Carella made it from the vehicle, trying to avoid looking at the bloody bodies, Bolan had gone through their pockets, finding nothing of any use. He opened the doors and checked the interior and again found it clean.

"Tell me something. How is it these bastards keep showing up?" Carella asked.

"We're dealing with people who do this for a living. With the right equipment it's easy to track someone. Use a credit card and they can access your account. Find out where and when the last transaction was made. Draw out cash from an ATM, the same applies. Security cameras pick you up and these people can see where you've been."

"Is this a subtle way of telling me we can't escape from Hoekken and his team?" Carella slumped against the side of the car. "Ordstrom is going to win, isn't he? Son of a bitch has everything on his side. Look how he found Ryan. Even found me here in Puerto Laredo." His voice rose. "Who do we trust, Cooper? *Who?*"

"Right now we don't trust anyone except each other. Not until I can get you somewhere safe."

"*Safe?* Where's safe? I came to Puerto Laredo because I didn't think anyone would find me. But they did. Cooper, we are being squeezed into a box so that Hoekken can walk in and take those files from my hand. Maybe I should call Ordstrom and tell him I quit. Let him have the damned files before there are any more pointless killings."

"You think he'll take them and thank you? Send you home with a pat on the head? Frank, as long as you're alive you're a threat to him. Even without the files you could cause him problems. Quit and he'll wipe you out on the spot. Then he *has* won. Is that what you want, Frank? Tell me if it is and we'll phone Ordstrom right now."

Carella shook his head. "Hell, no. I'm not about to give that bastard the satisfaction of seeing me quit."

"Then let's move. Get the hell away from here in case Hoekken has a backup team."

"That's a comforting thought."

"Not so much *comfort* when it's probably true."

"Is that why you've been collecting all the spare ordnance?"

Bolan nodded. "Something like that."

They climbed in the bullet-scarred 4x4 and Bolan got them back on the main trail, heading down towards the flatland.

Carella was silent for a time, gathering his thoughts. Bolan left him until the man chose to speak.

"I need some answers now, Cooper."

"Go ahead," the Executioner replied.

"Is Lesley okay?"

"Right now she's being looked after by my people. She's safe."

"How did she figure out where I was? I didn't tell her."

"She picked up some background noise when you called her from Puerto Laredo."

"Background noise? What the hell did she…?" Casper suddenly grinned. "The town band! She heard the town band. They were playing in the square when I phoned. I had so much on my mind it didn't register. That band is so out of tune."

"Smart lady."

"I called my sister, as well. You got any news on her?"

Bolan had been waiting for that one. As he heard Casper speak he took a breath and told it the only way he knew how.

"They got to her, Frank, before we knew where she was located. No easy way to say it. Veronica is dead. They killed her."

Carella's indrawn sob was loud enough to be heard over the sound of the 4x4's motor. He pressed back against the seat's padded headrest, staring straight out through the windshield. He stayed that way for some time, fists clenching and unclenching in his lap.

"And that's how Hoekken would have found out about Puerto Laredo. Apart from Lesley and me, she was the only other person who knew it was our hideaway." He gave a muffled groan. "They must have traced my call. Sweet Jesus, I led them to her. It's my fault she's dead."

"No. Frank, it wasn't your fault. Ordstrom's people would have found out where you were one way or another. We're dealing with a high profile organization. Tracking down someone wouldn't be difficult for them."

"Why kill her? What the hell did that achieve? God, she must have been so scared. Do you know what they did to her? I hope she talked before they hurt her too badly…."

Bolan let him talk. There was nothing he could do or say that would lessen the pain. Carella was blaming himself for leading Ordstrom's people to his sister. She had paid the ultimate price and Carella was taking the fallout.

Bolan was not surprised at the actions of Ordstrom's people. It was an attitude he had come across before. Ordstrom wanted results. His orders would have been explicit. *Do whatever is needed to safeguard our security. If people get hurt it doesn't matter. We're important. They are not. If they get in the way chop them down like weeds. But get results.*

Carella didn't say a word during the next half hour. Bolan knew the man would be going over everything that had happened and would be attempting to make sense of it all. His life, his world, had been permanently altered. One action leading to another, gathering speed as it went, and reaching the position where nothing seemed capable of stopping the wild ride. Friends and now family had been drawn into the affair. Death had visited Frank Carella. It was a harsh reality to have to face. There was no turning the clock back. Carella had committed himself once he decided to expose OTG's deceits. If he wanted inner peace, on one level at least, then he had to keep moving forward. Mack Bolan did not envy the man his choices. But he understood. He had been faced with the same dilemma himself at the beginning of his own personal odyssey. The Executioner had chosen to go forward and confront the enemy. He had never once regretted that decision.

18

Bolan pulled up beside the Dodge, which was parked outside the hotel. He leaned across to check the other vehicle. Empty. Casper, he figured, could be inside the hotel waiting. The image of the pilot nursing a cold beer flashed across his mind. Still, he did not open his door. Instead he took a long, slow look around the town plaza. It looked normal enough. People moving around. A few parked vehicles, mostly old American models. A radio playing from an upstairs window.

"Cooper?" Carella's voice had an uneasy edge to it. As if he had picked up Bolan's cautious mood. He reached out and touched Bolan's arm. "Something wrong?"

"I think we both need a cold beer," Bolan said.

He opened his door and stepped out, the Uzi held close to his side as he monitored Carella's own exit. He gestured for the man to join him at the front of the 4x4, staying close to Carella as they moved to the steps and made for the hotel entrance. No one took any particular notice of them, despite their untidy appearance and the weapon Bolan was carrying. Once they crossed the sidewalk and stepped into the hotel entrance they were shaded from the hot sun. The coolness of the lobby eased itself around them. Ahead was the desk. No one stood behind it. To the right he saw the arched doorway that led into the bar. If the town square had been quiet the inside of the hotel was almost tomblike in its silence. The only thing Bolan could hear was the soft sound of ceiling fans slowly rotating.

"Señor Pascal? Bud?"

Carella, slightly ahead of Bolan, had edged to one side so he could see around the arch, into the bar.

"Someone in there," he said.

"Frank," Bolan warned.

It was too late.

The man who stepped around the archway had a heavy automatic pistol in a beefy fist. The muzzle was coming in line with Carella's torso.

Bolan sidestepped, lunged at Carella and slammed his shoulder against the man. Carella was knocked sideways an instant before the pistol fired. The bullet cored into his right arm, above the elbow, spinning Carella off balance.

As Carella started to fall, the Uzi in Bolan's hands released a short burst that caught the shooter in the chest. The guy stumbled back, stopped short by the wall. Bolan was turning away from him as the shooter went down, leaving bloody stains on the white wall behind him.

Carella was on his knees, clutching his bleeding arm, his face white from shock. The Executioner grabbed him by the collar and dragged him to cover against the wall, ignoring the man's groans. Standing over him, Bolan checked the bar interior. No one was behind the counter. He could see the chairs stacked on the small tables.

He could also see Bud Casper, hunched over on one of the tall bar stools, leaning against the edge of the polished counter. Bolan could see the blood streaking Casper's face. Pascal was lying on the floor at Casper's feet, barely moving. His white suit and shirtfront were a mass of red, his face badly battered.

Bolan's observations took less than a couple of seconds. His reaction was even swifter as he picked up a shadow of movement on the far side of the bar. It was the sliver of light on a silver bracelet. Bolan stepped away from the arch, his Uzi rising. As his physical presence registered, the distant shadow turned into the shape of an armed figure, the man stepping away from the partition to make his shot. The weapon in Bolan's hands settled on the target, trigger already easing back. The crackle of sound was loud in the bar. The fusillade of 9 mm slugs ripped into the gunman's stomach, soft flesh yielding to the hard burn of the projectiles. The hit man went into a crouch, dropped his weapon and gripped his burning body.

The Executioner was moving on, picking up a second shooter, hearing the stutter of gunfire that sent a stream of slugs across the room. The shots met empty air as Bolan dropped to one knee the moment he registered the shooter. His Uzi curved around, spewing shots that hit home with deadly accuracy, sending the target crashing into a stacked table and chairs. He followed the chairs to the floor, gasping in agony as the bullets cored in deeply, and then Bolan hit him with a second burst that took pieces from his skull and left him twitching in brief, silent agony.

A third shooter rose into view from his hiding place behind the bar, pulling his weapon on line as Bolan surged into the room. His aim might have been better if Bud Casper had not taken the opportunity to join the fray. The pilot braced himself on one hand, the other reaching out to grasp a bottle from the counter. He slammed the heavy glass against the would-be shooter's skull, the impact enough to shatter both bone and glass. Casper struck again with the broken bottle, ramming the jagged ends into the shooter's throat. Blood spurted in a glistening fountain and the shooter dropped from sight. Casper had the presence of mind to snatch up the discarded submachine gun from the counter.

"Hey, Striker, you took your time," Casper said. He winced at the pain that creased his bloody face. "Ease off. They're all accounted for. But they were waiting for incoming reinforcements."

Bolan crouched beside Pascal. The Mexican man had taken

a severe beating. Apart from his face, one hand had also been crushed.

"Those boys had a nasty streak. Laid into him real bad," Casper said. "He just told 'em to go to hell when they started asking him questions."

"When you got here did you find a doctor?"

"Yeah. He's across the plaza."

"You okay to fetch him?" Bolan asked.

"No problem." Casper paused. "Did *you* find Carella?"

Bolan nodded.

"Over there. He caught a bullet, so tell the medic he's about to have a busy day."

Bolan helped Pascal into a chair. The Mexican had recovered enough to recognize him.

"Is Frank safe?" he asked.

"He's alive. It looks like we've brought you nothing but trouble, my friend."

Pascal formed a bloody smile. "And I have been complaining that in Puerto Laredo, nothing ever happens." He gripped Bolan's arm. "These are bad men. Are there more of them coming?"

"Seems likely. So we'll get out of here ASAP."

"If we could help."

"You've done enough. I won't put you in more danger. This is my problem. I'll handle it."

A commotion in the lobby attracted Bolan's attention. He turned and saw two uniformed men, drawn guns in their hands. They entered the bar, weapons aimed at Bolan.

Pascal raised a hand, speaking to the police officers. His words eased the situation and he introduced Puerto Laredo's police chief to Bolan. The man, Ortega, lean and sharp-eyed, nodded briefly. He instructed his officer to see where Casper and the doctor were.

"You must appreciate my position, Señor Cooper," the

police chief said in English. "This is a quiet town. Not used to such things. These people—" he waved a hand in the direction of the bodies "—this is not our way."

"I understand," Bolan said. "I want nothing more than to take this problem away. As soon as I have Carella seen to by the doctor we will leave. I regret what has happened but it was forced on me by circumstance."

"And how did you arrive here?"

"By plane. It's at Deaga Soterro's landing strip."

The Executioner stepped behind the bar, searching the shelves. He found a stack of clean bar towels, grabbed some and went to Carella. The man was still slumped against the wall, hugging his damaged arm. Bolan gently eased Carella's bloody hand away from the wound. The bullet had torn through flesh and muscle, breaking bone that was visible through the torn flesh. Bolan carefully wound a couple of towels around the bleeding mess.

"Best I can do until Bud gets back with the doc."

Carella, his face beaded with sweat, nodded. He used his good hand to indicate the backpack he was wearing.

"Inside," he said. "The files. I want you to take them, Cooper. In case I don't get out."

"You're getting out, Frank." Bolan smiled. "You think I came all this way to go home empty-handed?"

"Just take the damn files, Cooper. I have a feeling you can do more good with them than I ever could."

Bolan eased the pack off Carella's shoulders and opened it. He found clothing, personal items and a small metal container. Sliding the top back he saw two data flash drives nestled on a foam pad.

"Enough on there to sink Ordstrom and his cronies without a trace," Carella said.

Bolan closed the container and placed it in an inner pocket of his leather jacket, closing the zipper.

He heard footsteps crossing the lobby. Pushing to his feet he saw his pilot accompanied by a thin Mexican man clutching a medic pack. Ortega's officer, his handgun drawn, was close behind. Casper spoke to the doctor and the man knelt beside Carella and began to deal with the wounded arm.

"Bud?" Bolan said.

"Not good, Striker. There's a chopper coming in across the bay and we've got another four-by-four sitting on the other side of the plaza. Four armed guys are paying extra attention to where we are sitting right now. Something tells me they're not looking the place over with a view to booking in."

"Tell the doc to strap Carella's arm tight so we can move him. Give him a shot for the pain."

"Striker?"

"Do it, Bud. No time for anything else but to move. Just get him on his feet and ready to go."

Bolan turned, heading for the lobby exit.

"What the hell are you going to do?" the pilot called out.

The Executioner's parting words were sharp and to the point. "Whatever it takes."

19

Bolan stepped outside. The town plaza had suddenly become deserted. Above the bay he spotted the helicopter lazily moving in toward Puerto Laredo. The 4x4 Casper had mentioned was on the far side of the plaza. Two armed men stood beside the vehicle and he could make out hunched figures seated inside. Bolan didn't break stride as he crossed to where the Dodge sat. He opened one of the back doors and reached for the large bag that contained his additional arsenal. As he opened the bag he heard the burst of sound as the 4x4's motor was fired up. Bolan carried on with what he was doing.

He picked out an M-4 with an M-203 40 mm grenade launcher beneath the barrel assembly. Bolan snapped in a 30-round magazine, opened the launcher and loaded an HE round. As he stepped away from the Dodge he cocked the M-4, selected three-round burst capability and targeted the oncoming 4x4. The men who'd been standing beside the 4x4 were starting to advance. Windows had been lowered and Bolan saw other armed figures leaning out, weapons tracking him.

He raised the M-4, picked his target and fired the grenade. It struck the right front corner of the 4x4, the explosion ripping away a section of the hood. The force of the blast took out the windshield and turned the driver and front passenger into charred flesh and bone. Thick smoke curled out from the mangled twist of metal. The outside shooters were caught up in the blast. They were blown across the plaza, helpless in the grip of the fiery burst. Chunks of debris blew out from the impact area, clattering across the stone slabs. As the crippled vehicle lurched to a stop, the front end dropped to the ground and the rear doors flew open, disgorging the backseat riders.

The Executioner had dropped to a combat crouch, the M-4 to his shoulder as he hit the advancing shooters with precise tri-bursts. He caught the first guy as he emerged from drifting curls of smoke, the 5.56 mm slugs driving the guy to the ground in a twisting heap. The surviving shooter started to trigger his own weapon, sending choppy fire in Bolan's general direction, but he was making the classic error others had before—firing on full auto while on the move. It was a tactic not advised if accuracy was expected as the end result. Slugs bounced off the stone slabs of the plaza. The closest were a couple of yards from Bolan's position, and he remained where he was, holding his target until he picked his moment and fired. The shooter went down with a howl of pain, slugs ripping through his upper thigh. He pitched forward, his face scraping flesh against the rough stone, but he made a second attempt to put shots into Bolan. That effort earned him a second burst from the M-4 that took off the top of his skull.

Bolan stood, turning, and saw Casper, supporting Carella, moving out of the hotel. Ortega was behind them, surveying the scene of devastation. He raised his eyes to the oncoming helicopter, watching as it angled over to put it in line with the smoking 4x4.

Casper had moved Carella to the Dodge, opened the back door and helped the man inside. The Mexican doctor had bound his wounded arm tight to his side, wrapping a swathe of bandage around Carella's torso to hold it immobile.

"I will handle things here, Señor Cooper," Ortega said. "I suggest you leave now." The tone he used confirmed it was not a suggestion, but an order. *"Ir rápidamente."*

Bolan climbed behind the wheel of the Dodge, started the motor and turned the wheel as the vehicle burned rubber across the plaza. He retraced the way they had come in, pushing the gas pedal down hard, and felt the powerful engine boost up the speed. The Dodge thundered through the narrow streets, bouncing as it hit uneven patches, tires squealing as Bolan hit the brakes on sharp curves. As the houses flashed by and the road curved through open terrain Bolan increased his speed.

Casper had his window down, craning his neck to check the incoming helicopter. Now he eased back inside.

"He's on our tail. Some way behind but he's coming." He bent over to inspect Bolan's cache of weapons. "You got anything in here to knock that thing out the sky?"

Bolan grabbed the M-4 from the passenger seat and thrust it back at Casper. "Best we've got."

Casper bent over the weapons bag again. He came out with more HE grenades for the M-203 and two additional magazines for the M-4.

"You just drive, 'cause I am ready to do some serious harm if that eggbeater gets close enough," Casper said.

"If this thing had seat belts I'd advise you to buckle up. It hasn't, so just hang on," the Executioner replied.

Bolan's advice was sound. The road surface didn't lend itself to high speed driving and the Dodge 4x4 had its suspension well tested. A thick trail of dust marked their passing. Bolan realized it would help the chopper's pilot keep them in sight. There was nothing else he could do.

The crackle of auto fire reached his ears. Gouts of the hard-packed dirt flew into the air, short of the Dodge, rattling against the back end. There was a pause, then more firing. This burst hit the right side of the road.

"Sometime soon that old boy on the trigger is going to have our range," Casper murmured.

"You ready with your piece?" Bolan asked.

"Sure. Why?"

Bolan's answer was to stand on the brake pedal. The Dodge

bucked and slithered as forward velocity fought with brake power. The dark bulk of the helicopter overshot them. Casper leaned out of his side window and loosed off a long burst aimed at the chopper's underside. He did hear one metallic *ping* as a slug hit the fuselage.

The helicopter pilot banked sharply, taking the bird out of range as he flew in a wide circle.

Bolan powered up again, gripping the wheel as the Dodge picked up speed. From the corner of his eye he could see the helicopter making its long sweep around.

"He's coming back, Bud."

"I got him in my sights."

"I hope so," Carella said between clenched teeth. It was the first time he had spoken since leaving Puerto Laredo.

"He's coming in," Casper shouted.

The vicious chatter of the helicopter's weapon reached them. A ragged line of shots gouged the earth. Hard grit rattled the side of the Dodge. Bolan worked the wheel, sending the speeding vehicle back and forth across the narrow road. Dust rose in thick clouds. The downdraft from the swooping chopper created even more, the swirling coils nearly blinding Bolan's vision. The helicopter pilot was almost overhead, the dark bulk blocking the light.

"Son of a bitch is too close. His gunner can't reach us," Casper shouted above the noise. "What the hell is he doing?"

"His mistake," Bolan said. "Let's make use of it."

Casper leaned out the side window again, angling the M-4 up at the chopper's underside and triggered a burst that ripped into the alloy fuselage. The helicopter side slipped, not gaining much height. Bolan saw it from the corner of his eye. The aircraft was pulling away and he realized the opportunity they were presented with.

"Use the grenade, Bud. Hit him *now*."

Casper brought the M-4 around, turning the muzzle on the

bulk of the machine. His finger activated the grenade and it burst from the launcher. For Casper it was like watching a slow motion movie. The faint trail behind the grenade tracked its progress, which in reality was no more than a few seconds. He could have sworn he saw the moment of impact. Then the grenade detonated against the fuselage, the bright flare of the explosion blossoming and spreading out. The initial detonation expanded into a harsh crackle of sound, the chopper splitting apart and becoming a ball of fire suspended in the air. Shock waves rippled out and caught the Dodge, almost turning it on its side. Debris rained down, slamming against the vehicle as Bolan struggled to keep it moving, flooring the gas pedal to send it surging forward, away from the disintegrating helicopter as it lost its struggle with gravity. Its forward motion carried the broken aircraft even after it slammed into the ground. Parts hurled in every direction. They smashed through the underbrush, and splintered trees, creating a number of small fires.

Bolan brought the vehicle to a stop. He climbed out and walked back to stare at the downed helicopter. Smoke was rising in a coiling cloud over the wreck. Something moved within the tangle of twisted metal—a jerking, ungainly form, struggling to free itself from its surroundings. It lurched free, then took a few faltering steps before it dropped facedown on the fire-blackened earth.

"That bastard Ordstrom is responsible for too many people dying," Casper said. "Too damn many, Striker."

"His account is going to be settled," Bolan said as he turned back to the Dodge. "Sooner than he thinks."

20

The man walking into the room was dressed in civilian clothing, but his stance told Ordstrom he was military. He carried a leather briefcase in his left hand.

"Should I know you?" Ordstrom asked.

"Thomas Randisi, sir. From Camp Macklin, Texas."

"Of course. Excuse my ignorance, Sergeant Randisi, but we have never actually met."

"I imagine, Mr. Ordstrom, you won't have met most of the people on your payroll."

Ordstrom wasn't sure how to take the man's remark. He studied Randisi's solid features, coming to the conclusion that the soldier was simply stating a fact. There was no slight in his manner.

"My organization is large and diverse. A little like the army, Sergeant Randisi. And you are right. People have been hired and fired without my ever meeting them." Ordstrom pushed to his feet. "Excuse my manners. Would you like a drink? Maybe coffee? Take a seat."

Randisi declined the refreshments but took one of the leather seats facing Ordstrom's desk.

"Bad business out there," Ordstrom said, resuming his own seat. "It would seem you are the only one who walked away from it all. But not without some damage," he added, staring at Randisi's bruised face.

"To give the man his due, he could handle himself."

"But you did get away."

"One of the things they teach you in the army, sir. Evasion. How to slip away before the net is closed. After the incident at the camp I figured if I wanted to stay clear of the investigation I had to quit the place. When that so-called CID colonel went after your man Janssen I had to make a quick decision."

Something clicked in Ordstrom's mind as Randisi spoke. "*You* shot Janssen."

"It was a field decision, Mr. Ordstrom. Janssen would have talked. Given Stone everything he knew."

Ordstrom had known Stefan Janssen. The man had been good at his job but lacked backbone. Janssen would definitely have given up his knowledge if he had been arrested.

"A good call, Sergeant."

"Problem was I didn't make the follow-through. I took Stone prisoner but he got away, killing Bosley in the process."

"I received some reports on what went down. Something tells me you can fill in the blanks."

Randisi placed the briefcase on Ordstrom's desk. He opened it and took out a slim laptop computer and files of documents.

"We didn't keep any data on camp computers. Or paper records. All compromising material was handled by Janssen. That's his laptop. These files hold all the hard copy details. I was able to retrieve everything before anyone figured out what was going on at the base."

"I can see why Janssen recruited you in the first place. Smart thinking, Randisi. I won't forget this."

"Somebody had to use their brains back there. If I'd left it to Bosley I'd be in a cell by now."

"That doesn't have the touch of respect I might have expected," Ordstrom said.

"Respect is something that has to be earned," Randisi said. "It's not a God-given right. Even when we're talking about colonels. Bosley never did anything to earn my respect."

"He *was* your commanding officer."

Randisi smiled. "He was a dumb ass-kisser, Mr. Ordstrom. Simple as that. He took your money, but when it came to the cut he screwed up. Stone did us all a favor when he kicked Bosley's flabby ass out of that chopper. Have you tracked Stone down?" Randisi asked.

"As far as I've been able to learn, Stone doesn't exist. I had my sources in the military run him through the database. There's no information on Stone. Army CID shows nothing."

"So how did the son of a bitch make it to Camp Macklin? With all the credentials he needed. And intel on Bosley and me? Someone must have fed him that."

Ordstrom nodded in agreement. "The first name I thought of was Colonel Dane Nelson."

"Francis Nelson's old man?"

"The Francis Nelson you took care of because he was getting too close."

"Yeah, I know who he was. Don't forget I was the one who dropped the hammer on that nosy bastard."

"You've been a busy man, Sergeant Randisi."

Randisi smiled. "I like to earn my pay."

"It did strike me this Stone character must have been the one who interfered when that hit on Dane Nelson went wrong after his son's funeral."

"That's what happens when you use amateurs, Mr. Ordstrom."

"I would hardly class Hoekken as an *amateur*."

Randisi smiled. "Pardon my French, but he hasn't exactly pulled off the operation of the fucking century. I talked to my OTG guy over the phone and the way he told it suggested things haven't been running the way you want. Way I heard it, Hoekken sends his people out and just seems to add to OTG's body count. Now he's somewhere in Mexico, still trying to lay his hands on this guy Carella. Coming up minus more crew members, and Stone and Carella are still alive."

Ordstrom could not argue the point. The failure of Hoekken's not inconsiderable force was becoming an embarrassment. The South African head of OTG's security division had not delivered as promised. Ordstrom was still hoping the man could complete his assignment and return the missing data files. If he did not and Carella managed to get the information into neutral hands, where Ordstrom had no influence, then OTG, which included Ordstrom himself, and the individuals aligned with him, would be in real trouble.

Ordstrom was a powerful man, with wide-ranging contacts and influence. He was not vain enough to believe he could get away without blame. The domino effect, too, was a viable scenario.

So he needed to back up his backup. In the end Ordstrom's priorities were slanted toward himself. It was a logical and expected consideration. His life had been based on his own survival, first and foremost. The current situation lent itself to those criteria. If he, Ordstrom, went to the wall, others would follow. So his actions needed to follow that path.

"I'm glad you decided to come here, Randisi."

"I was limited in choice," Randisi said. "Going AWOL tends to shorten the options."

"Don't concern yourself with that. We can work around it. I have connections. Most of the main agencies. Law enforcement. My military contacts can make your absence from your unit go away. In the meantime maybe I can make use of your experience."

"Why?"

"Like it or nor, we are in this together. That data has to be suppressed. I want you to find and terminate Carella and that interfering bastard Stone. You have as much riding on this as

I do, Thomas. Stone is still a threat. I'd like someone like you between us."

Randisi grinned. "I like a man who doesn't pretend he's doing something simply out of concern for someone other than himself."

"The instinct for survival is endemic in us all. Let's look at it as a joint venture. We can both survive if we ensure Stone and Carella are put down."

"And what else do I get apart from saving my skin?"

"Freedom from any form of military comeback. A new identity if you need. I can make those things happen. Large cash bonus."

"Negotiable. What about the present? I had to walk out on my life in the clothes on my back. If I'm going after Stone and Carella I'll need things."

"No problem. Tell me what you need and I'll organize it."

"Weapons?"

"Of course. Anything you want. This *is* OTG."

Randisi reached for a notepad and wrote down his requirements. He slid the pad across the desk and waited as Ordstrom read the list.

"Quite Spartan. Are you certain this is all you need?"

"I've been a soldier for a long time, Mr. Ordstrom. I can operate with a minimum of equipment. I don't have time for life's luxuries right now. You get me what's on that list, see if you can pinpoint Hoekken's last location, and I'll handle the rest."

"Do you need any backup?"

"When the army sent me out on a sniper detail the most I ever had with me was a spotter. Plenty of times not even that luxury. If I decide I want physical help there are men I can call on."

"Military? Ex-military?"

Randisi didn't say a word. He just tilted his head. "Right now the only other thing I want on top of the list is transport."

"Fair enough."

Ordstrom picked up a phone, made a connection and began to give orders. His tone allowed no queries. He was on the line for no more than five minutes. When he finished he nodded to Randisi.

"There will be a car waiting outside by the time you reach the door. It will take you to the plant. By the time you arrive everything you need will be waiting for you. One of my people will meet you—Rick Weatherby. He's been instructed to give you anything you want, no questions asked. He should also be able to update you on Hoekken's whereabouts. I'll let you handle it from there. Thomas, I hope I can rely on *you*. Hoekken assured me he had the situation under control. It appears my faith in him was ill judged. Just do it right this time."

"I'll be in touch, Mr. Ordstrom."

"In the meantime I'll be using my connections to monitor any attempts by Carella to make contact. We'll cover agencies, the police. Mr. Carella is going to find the world can be a very small place. He made a big mistake when he decided to take me on."

"His choice, sir," Randisi said, turning to leave the room.

Ordstrom crossed to the window and saw Randisi emerge from the house and step into the limousine waiting for him. As the car drove away another vehicle rolled along the driveway, coming to a stop outside the front door. Ordstrom watched the two men climb from the back and enter the house. He turned from the window and crossed the room to meet his new guests.

Two important members of the group, who were as much part of the organization as Ordstrom himself, had arrived.

The last time they had met had been under better circumstances. This time around, lighthearted banter would play no part in their conversation.

21

"I thought we were hiring the best local people," Hoekken raged. "How could they get themselves shot down by a man in a fucking four-by-four?"

As his anger increased, his Afrikaans accent became stronger. No one made any comment. Hoekken was angry enough to strike out at anyone who got too close. It wouldn't have been the first time. His temper was legendary. Arnold Hoekken drove himself without letup and expected the same dedication from anyone working for him.

"Last thing we heard from Chavez was that the pilot had been buzzing the vehicle," Sawyer said. "They took some small arms fire and the pilot turned away. Chavez radioed the shooter in the Dodge had an auto rifle with a tube under the barrel. Then he yelled to the pilot to get them clear just before a loud noise. The radio connection went dead—"

"Grenade launcher," Hoekken said. "They hit the chopper with an HE round." He cast around the hangar they were using as their base in Mexico. "This is getting out of hand. All we have to do is take down that fuck Carella. But all I'm getting are reports that some Lone Ranger has joined up with him and he's putting down our people like a turkey shoot." He took a long, deep breath, calming himself before he spoke again. "How is that possible, Sawyer? *Eh?* Tell me how one man can just walk in and start wiping out our help?"

Sawyer shrugged. "We can't get a line on him, Mr.

Hoekken. The only thing we did find out was he called himself Colonel Brandon Stone when he showed up at Camp Macklin. Supposed to be from Army CID, but when our contact checked him out the guy didn't exist. He'd been given clearance and ID through Colonel Dane Nelson."

"Damned son of his who was working with Ryan and started this thing off. So Nelson hires this bastard to make things right for his son and Stone turns it into a full-scale war."

"Nelson must be paying him well."

Hoekken shook his head. "I think there's more to it. This Stone is more than just a gun-for-hire. The man has military experience. He's too good for a local hit man. *We're* hiring the amateurs and he's cutting through them like a fucking combat unit. I'm thinking this fella is ex-military himself. Look at the way he bluffed himself into Camp Macklin. Talked his way through Bosley and he even fooled Randisi at the start. The way Randisi spoke the guy had military presence. Shit, man, you can't learn that in five minutes."

"He screwed our deal at Macklin. Took Bosley out of the picture and forced Randisi to go AWOL."

"Ordstrom has that in hand. He can make Janssen the guilty party at Camp Macklin. That's the easy part. Ordstrom puts out the word to his connections and OTG will be cleared of anything to do with the setup."

"But even Ordstrom won't be able to shrug off the information in Carella's files. They could still bring the whole thing down," Sawyer pointed out. "And burn some higher-ups in the process."

"Then we don't let Carella hand over those files." Hoekken turned to face the waiting crew. "Get that other chopper in the air. Find those bastards and eliminate them." He snapped his fingers at Sawyer. "Get me Ordstrom on the sat-phone. The secure number. Do it, man."

Sawyer opened the attaché case that contained the sat-phone. He tapped in the lock code, waited for a connection, then punched in the appropriate numbers. As soon as the dial-out began he handed the phone to Hoekken and walked away to give the man privacy.

"GODDAMN IT, ARNIE, we can't allow that little runt to beat us. Fine, we have him on the run, but as long as he has those files he's got us by the balls," Ordstrom said.

"I'm on it," Hoekken said. "I admit I underestimated this bloke Carella has helping him. The guy is good. But there's one thing that makes him vulnerable. He's human. Not a fucking robot. He *can* be killed."

"Then I suggest you do just that, Arnie. Wipe them both off the face of the planet. If you have to burn up half of Mexico to achieve that, do it. The last thing I want are the Feds knocking on my door. Right now I have to go and smooth some ruffled feathers. One or two of our associates are on the verge of soiling their pants. Talk with you later, Arnie, and please have some good news for me."

Ordstrom replaced the receiver. He crossed to look out of the window, across the well-tended lawn and gardens that graced the wide expanse behind his house. The day was bright, the sun warm. The only thing to sour it was the continuing problem exacerbated by Frank Carella.

Damn the man.

Why couldn't he simply curl up and die, taking those files with him? Their removal would end this continuing nightmare. And that was what it was.

A waking nightmare that refused to go away.

Everything had been rolling along nicely before Cal Ryan and his accomplice, Carella, had uncovered data that had supposedly been deleted from the OTG computer database. Part of that data had implicated Janssen, the OTG link man at Camp Macklin, in Texas, who along with the base commander, Bosley, and Master Sergeant Randisi, had been working deals for OTG. Ryan had informed a young army lieutenant, Francis Nelson, a longtime friend. When Nelson had started snooping around Camp Macklin, Randisi had overreacted and tracked him to Washington and killed him. That had not been the end. A colonel from Army CID had shown up at the camp, looking into allegations of misconduct and asking questions. From there everything at Camp Macklin went down the toilet. Bosley was dead. Randisi had gone AWOL, eventually showing up at Ordstrom's home and working a deal with him. The CID colonel had turned out to be anything but genuine. Since Camp Macklin the man kept showing up and putting down Ordstrom's teams. Despite Arnold Hoekken's experience and skill, Stone—or whoever he was—kept handling whatever stood in his way.

Not an ideal situation, especially considering what was at stake. All that brought Ordstrom to the meeting he had to face there and then. He heard a tap on the door and knew the moment had arrived.

"Yes?"

The door opened and his manservant stood there.

"Your guests have arrived, sir. They are in the main room."

"Fine, Edward. I'm on my way."

"I took the liberty of offering them drinks."

Ordstrom nodded. "Whatever they're having, make mine a double."

"Of course, sir."

Ordstrom made his way to the large room that overlooked the front garden. His two guests, dressed in expensive casual clothing, clutched large tumblers of his finest single malt whiskey.

"This early in the day?" Ordstrom said lightly.

"Considering the reason we're here, Jacob, I should be taking it directly from the bottle."

Colonel David J. Kindred, U.S. Army, worked out of the Pentagon. He was a man of expensive tastes who regarded his own survival and financial status to be the most important matters to pursue. Kindred had little time for those who simply sat back and did nothing to make the most from offered opportunities. Ordstrom saw him as a bore, with little to offer save for his considerable influence and a list of contacts as long as the Potomac.

"I'll have a couple of crates shipped to your yacht," Ordstrom said.

"I fail to see any humor in our situation. Ye gods, man, if this man Carella gets his information to the right people we are all going to be spending the rest of our lives in solitary, courtesy of the federal prison service," the second guest said.

Senator Mark Riesling sat on so many committees he spent most of his time moving from one to another. He chaired oversights into military spending and had his hand in contracts that ran into the billions of dollars. Riesling was a truly avaricious man who took so many kickbacks it was a miracle his behind wasn't permanently black and blue with bruises, Ordstrom thought. The man was also extremely devious and kept his backdoor dealings well concealed. He maintained a whiter-than-white public persona. He was a dedicated sponsor of charities and had a solid marriage that had lasted sixteen years. He also had a current mistress who lived in an expensive Washington apartment. He was a man never to be crossed. He did not forgive, nor forget, and had an ugly side to him that warned individuals not to cross him. Riesling was unaware of the evidence Ordstrom had concerning two incidents where the man had paid to have enemies worked over so badly one ended up in a wheelchair and the other still suffered from memory loss.

"Mark, I may not have the little prick in my hands right now, but he's on the run. Doesn't know where to go. Time is running out for him. My people are closing in even as we speak."

"Do I look like a contestant off a TV reality show? I am not a fucking idiot, Jacob. This is getting too close to the wire. Let's not dance around on this. We could end up in deep shit. I, for one, have no intention of letting that happen. For Christ's sake, between the three of us we should be able to bring thunder and lightning down on Carella."

"We have enough clout to be able to shut him off from any law enforcement agency," Kindred said. "And I'd like to get to that bastard running interference for him. He's good. Can't argue that point. And he's got *cojones.* Have to give him that. Son of a bitch waltzing in and out of an army base like that. At least we know the kind of man he is, even if his identity is a mystery."

"Has it been considered that he might be some kind of government covert agent?" Riesling asked.

"It's possible," Ordstrom said. "But unlikely. None of our sources have picked up any whispers. We kept this affair in-house, so to speak. Government has been shut out of the loop. If there had been any agency involvement there would have been spooks crawling out of the woodwork. But there is nothing. That's why we have to hold the lid down tight and get this cleared away quickly. I have my people on it because the leak came from OTG. I won't deny it. But I also will not go down without the fight of my life, because if Carella hands over those files the fallout will spread far and wide. And we all know what that means."

Riesling and Kindred had no need for that to be spelled out for them. If the data on the files was exposed the fall of OTG would reach out and taint them all. There would be fingers pointed and names named. Any investigation, once kick-started, would become a self-perpetuating organism. It would look into every deal. It would pick out the minutia of contracts and orders. The intricate web of deceit would start to unravel. Self-preservation would take over. Loyalty would become a personal matter.

It would not be a pleasant thing to witness.

Or be caught up in.

22

"Get us there. Quickly. I want to catch those bastards while they are in the open." Hoekken rounded on his team. "Let's do this right for once. No wonder those fucking Mexicans came cheap. You hire them by the dozen and not one of them is worth a ten-cent piece."

"Our guy in La Paz said they were the best."

Hoekken's laughter echoed around the cabin.

"The best? Those idiots were the best? God help the Mexican mob, then."

"Puerto Laredo on the right," the pilot said over the intercom. "I'm changing course now. Following Florio's heading before he went down."

Hoekken went forward and dropped into the seat beside the pilot. "Can't you get any more speed out of this thing?"

The pilot laid in more revs. Hoekken grunted in approval. He was leaning forward, peering through the windshield. His attention never once strayed from the ground flashing beneath them.

"There," he said, pointing. "Smoke. It's that damned chopper."

The pilot took them lower and they flew over the still-smoking wreckage of the downed helicopter.

"Can't be too far ahead," the pilot said. He was skimming the tops of the trees now, following the snaking course of the narrow road. It wasn't long before he spotted the drifting trail of dust.

"Up ahead."

Hoekken nodded.

"That's it," he said. "Man, look at the way he's moving. Damn, he knows we have him spotted. He'll run out of road if he isn't careful." He keyed his com-set. "Sawyer, you got that LAW ready?"

"Yeah."

"We'll go in on his backside. Soon as you have a solid lock you blow that Dodge apart."

The pilot descended quickly, bringing himself in line with the speeding vehicle. Hoekken heard the burst of wind as the side hatch slid open. He turned in his seat and saw that Sawyer, clipped to a harness, was kneeling in the open way, the LAW already in the firing position.

"Make it a good shot," Hoekken said.

Sawyer held his aim, then touched the trigger. The LAW belched its load. The rocket streaked from the tube and hit the ground no more than a foot behind the Dodge. Despite not being a direct hit the blast was enough to lift the truck, tear away much of the rear body and shred both back tires. The Dodge lurched, slid sideways, then turned over and began to cartwheel along the road, then bounced off the track. A trail of fire, smoke and thick dust marked its progress. The bulk of the careering vehicle tore through the undergrowth. It took down a number of smaller trees before it slammed into the solid trunk of a heavy tree and came to a sudden stop.

"Put us down," Hoekken ordered. "I want to be sure that bastard Carella is dead and I need to see those damned files. You wait here for us."

The chopper pilot had to fly around in a wide circle before he was able to find a suitable spot to put down. The minute the helicopter touched down, Hoekken and his three-man team were out of the aircraft, weapons locked and loaded as they pushed through the undergrowth in the direction of the rising smoke from the disabled truck.

Hoekken's anticipation of ending the hunt spurred him forward as he pushed through the deep foliage. The smoke was rising above the tree line. There was hardly any wind so it hung over the wrecked Dodge, and as Hoekken broke free of the undergrowth he waved his crew forward. "Go and check them."

The crackle of automatic fire came from thick brush to his right. Hoekken saw his lead man go down, his weapon firing into the earth as he fell. Close behind, Sawyer returned fire, his burst sending a stream of slugs into the undergrowth. The unseen shooter fired again, from a position yards away from the initial spot. Sawyer cried out as hot slugs burned into his flesh. He stumbled drunkenly, clutching at his shattered thighs, and as his knees touched the ground a second burst caught him in the head, tearing away the left side of his face.

"Move," Hoekken yelled at his surviving man.

The man did, angling away from the area. Hoekken himself began to backtrack. Gunfire sounded and the third crewman went down, stitched from his waist to a spot just below his shoulder blades. He was flung facedown on the ground, blood bursting from the wounds.

Hoekken dropped to a crouch, bringing up his pistol. He gripped it two-handed to steady his aim. He picked his spot and fired, the rounds cleaving through the undergrowth. Then he shifted the muzzle and fired again, feet to the right, then left.

No response.

Hoekken rose to his feet, a slight frown creasing his tanned face. He slid his left hand under his jacket and pulled out his second pistol. It was a habit he had developed some years ago. Having two weapons saved time reloading in an urgent situation. Saving time could mean the difference between living and dying. And with a man like this Stone there would be no leeway. He had proved his skill and his ability to survive. Hoekken heard one of his downed men groaning in pain. Stone had proved himself once again. He had walked away from the crash, taken out Hoekken's three shooters, and now he was waiting for his chance against Hoekken.

That seemed odd. Why was he waiting? All he had to do was pull the trigger and it would be over. Unless one of Hoekken's shots had found its target. Maybe Stone was dead, or badly wounded. Lying bleeding in the undergrowth. Unable to respond.

Not impossible. Hoekken had laid down a solid burst of spaced-out fire. All it took was one well-placed bullet.

One bullet.

Hoekken swapped weapons, the fully loaded one in his right hand. He was capable with his left hand, but not as good as with his right.

The brush to his extreme right rustled. Hoekken swung his pistol to cover the area. He felt sure he could see movement there.

"Stone. Come out, man. Show yourself."

The tall figure stepping into view was bruised and bloody, his clothing tattered and smoke-blackened from the crash. He had discarded the submachine gun and carried a big Desert Eagle in his right hand. Despite his appearance there was something in his stance that told Hoekken he was far from defeated. When he looked into the piercing blue eyes, Hoekken felt a moment of fear. It was something he had not experienced for many years.

Arnold Hoekken considered himself a seasoned fighter. The South African was a veteran of armed conflicts that spanned the globe. His time with OTG had been easy compared to some of the hot spots he had been in. Being head of security for the vast conglomerate had done little to challenge his skills. The Carella affair was the first time he had been required to call on his past experience. A fleeting moment of self-doubt flitted across his mind. Had he softened? Become too used to the comfort zone that OTG presented him with? His life had offered no real challenges.

Nothing to maintain his sharp edge. And the people he had working under him were not combat veterans. Certainly not at the level Hoekken would have wished. That fact was compounded by the fact they were all down on the ground, either dead or dying.

Well, Arnold, you picked them. Man, you picked wrong, he thought.

And you picked a hell of a man to stand against you.

He made up his mind in that brief moment of clarity. No waiting. No time-wasting. He was here to complete his mission and Stone was in his way.

It was inevitable. An inescapable fact that came down to a single realization.

Someone had to die.

Hoekken's finger pressed against the trigger, the muzzle of the Glock centering on Stone.

Hoekken felt a hard blow just above his eyes. It snapped his head back. His finger jerked the Glock's trigger, sending the shot skyward. The blow came from a .44 Magnum slug put between Hoekken's eyes. It was over and done in a heartbeat. Hoekken never even felt the passage of the slug as it cored through his brain and blew out the back of his skull.

The Executioner watched the man drop. A dead weight crumpling to the ground.

Hoekken's death was a signal for Bolan to briefly let go. He felt his abused body slump. Allowed the pain to surge. He might have fallen to the ground himself if there had not been the need to attend to others. Bolan holstered his weapon, then turned slowly and made his way back to where the wreck of the Dodge lay crumpled against the base of the tree. The doors were sagging open, sprung by the force of the final impact. Smoke drifted from the crumbled hood. The smell of burning, mingled with hot oil, reached Bolan's nostrils. He moved closer to the vehicle, picking up the sound of someone stirring inside the wreck.

Bud Casper leaned out from one of the open doors. He reached for support, missed it and tumbled from the seat. He landed hard, cursing loudly, struggling to right himself. At first glance it looked as if he had been coated in blood. It was streaming from a severe gash in his scalp, running freely down his face and soaking the front of his shirt. As Bolan closed in on him Casper raised his head, spitting blood from his mouth.

"I am going to double my rates for any future trips with you." The effort of speaking set him groaning and he clutched at his left side, sucking in breath through clenched teeth. "Tell me you have personal injury insurance. Especially for broken ribs."

"I'll check it out when we get back."

"Christ, I reckon that means *no* insurance."

Bolan slid his hands under Casper's arms and eased the pilot away from the Dodge, settling him with his back against a tree.

"Go check on Frank," Casper said. "He didn't look too good."

Bolan climbed back into the Dodge, leaning over Carella's still form. It didn't take him long to assess the man's condition. Carella was bloody, his body hunched over in a twisted shape. He was jammed between the front and back seats, his left leg at an awkward angle. The arm that had been strapped to his body was crushed beneath him, bone sticking out through the sodden bandage. The left side of his face was torn from just below his eye to his jawline, the flesh peeled back down to the muscle. Carella was unconscious, but there was still a faint pulse.

"He's alive, Bud, but he needs to be in a hospital," Bolan called.

"Those shooters landed in a chopper close by," Casper said. "If it's still waiting we could use it."

Bolan slid out of the Dodge. As he straightened, his body groaned in protest. He pulled the Desert Eagle and ejected the clip, snapping in a fresh one. He made his way back to where Casper lay, handing him the Beretta.

"I'll go and get us a ride," he said.

THE HELICOPTER PILOT sat waiting, a pistol in one hand. He wasn't sure what was happening. Since the brief round of gunfire it had gone quiet. He had seen the smoke rising from the crash site. Nothing else. His patience was wearing thin. Not that it made any difference. He was being paid to do the flying, so what the hell.

He didn't see or hear anything, so he was genuinely surprised when the battered and bloody figure appeared at his side of the cockpit, the muzzle of a huge pistol pointing at him.

"Lose the gun," Bolan said.

The pilot did what he was told. It had dawned quickly that if this man was here, alive, then Hoekken and his men were most likely dead. He lifted the pistol, ejected the magazine and worked the slide to empty the round from the breech.

"You got a med kit on board?"

"Yeah."

"Get it and climb down."

Bolan guided the pilot back to the crash site.

"Bud, keep him in your sights," Bolan said. "You come with me. We need to get someone out of the car."

When the pilot saw Carella's crumpled form he shook his head. "He won't make it."

"We still try," Bolan told him. "I won't let him die like this."

Between them they eased Frank Carella from the wreck. He only stirred once, groaning as he registered the pain, then went under again. They carried him to where Casper lay, placing him on the foil blanket from the med kit.

"Do you have any paramedic training?" Bolan asked.

"A little," the pilot said.

"Then use it to do what you can to stabilize them first."

"Before what?"

Casper managed a tired grin. "Before you evac us to a hospital back across the border."

The pilot glanced between Bolan and Casper. He realized

they were serious. And they were both well-armed. He figured he had no choice. So he pulled the med kit to him and got on with it, thinking that the day could not get any weirder.

23

"So what was Hoekken's last known location?" Randisi asked.

He was in one of the top-floor offices at OTG where the man assigned by Ordstrom to assist was bent over a state-of-the-art computer system. The computer was linked into the OTG mainframe, allowing access to the feed from Hoekken.

"I can show you his location the last time we spoke to him. It seems he was in pursuit of Carella and Stone. Hoekken said they were ready to take them out. There was a break in contact before the pilot called and said Hoekken and his men were on foot, making their way to the crash site to verify the hit."

"And then what?"

"Nothing," Rick Weatherby said. "We tried to reestablish contact but it didn't happen. We thought maybe there had been some kind of break in the signal. Went through the frequencies. There were no problems. We had to assume that the channel had been closed down."

Randisi considered the options. He could see no valid reason why Hoekken would stop transmitting. If the radio was still functioning why would he shut it off? He ran through the reasons, finally coming up with the only one that made any sense to him.

Hoekken was no longer in control of the radio. Or the chopper.

"Can you still track the helicopter?"

"Yes. It has a locator tracker on board. So it can be located in an emergency. They're built in during construction."

"Tell me where it is right now."

Weatherby worked at the keyboard. The monitor displayed a series of chart overlays, finally showing a steady image. A small red dot appeared, moving imperceptibly.

"The helicopter is in the air. It just flew across the border, back into California airspace."

"Can you pinpoint where it lands?"

"Yes."

"Okay. I want the OTG executive jet warmed up and ready to go when I arrive. Stay in contact and advise of the chopper's destination once I'm airborne. It has to touch down sooner or later. My guess is somewhere in California. Inform Mr. Ordstrom. Keep him in the loop."

FORTY MINUTES LATER Randisi was seated in the OTG corporate jet as it winged its way from the private airfield some miles from the main plant. His equipment had been loaded onboard. Randisi had an open phone line to OTG so he could stay in contact with Rick Weatherby.

Two hours into the flight, Weatherby spoke to Randisi.

"The chopper put down a while ago."

"Where?"

"In the grounds of a local hospital. Ideal setup. Small town. Small hospital."

"Can you hack into their patient database? Don't say yes unless you mean it."

Weatherby laughed. "We manufacture surveillance equipment here at one of the OTG divisions. We can pretty well look at and listen to whatever you want."

"Then do it. If those targets are in that hospital find out exactly who they are and where they are."

"I can bring in one of the techs. Use the hospital's online systems."

"Do it. Ordstrom's orders are anything I need. I *need* this guy."

"What are we looking for?"

"Admissions that fit the time frame. If it's Carella or Stone, they won't be there under their own names. Just come up with probables. Get back to me when you have something. Ask your guy to get into the security camera system. See if he can pick up images. Get him to run them through OTG's personnel files. If he can get a match to Carella we're in business."

"That shouldn't be a problem."

Settling back in his seat Randisi tuned out. There was nothing else he could do during the flight but wait for results. In the interim he decided to get some rest. The old military adage dictated that between engagements, if there was nothing else to do, sleep and food were the best options. Take it while the chance presented itself because it could be a long time before you got the offer again.

The buzzing of the phone roused him. Randisi checked his watch. He had been asleep for almost an hour. He picked up. "Talk to me."

"We've got them. Three people came from the helicopter. One needed to be gurneyed inside. The others were walking wounded. According to the admissions data the lead guy showed ID as a Justice agent. Matt Cooper. He was with a Bud Casper. The injured one went in as a John Doe. But he's Frank Carella. No doubt. You have a computer station onboard. Go to it and log on."

As the monitor came to life, Randisi followed Weatherby's phone instructions.

"The hospital has a digital security system. Means any images are pretty sharp. My tech was able to pick up the three as they entered the hospital. Images were logged on different cameras as they progressed through. The guy on the gurney was the hardest to catch, but there was a full face shot just before they took him through to the treatment room. We fed it into our databank here and it came up with a ten-point identification. It's Frank Carella. No question."

"Did you get a shot of Cooper?"

An image filled the monitor screen. Head and shoulders. Thick dark hair above a serious face still streaked with blood and bruises. The eyes were unforgettable.

"You son of a bitch, Stone," Randisi said softly.

"You know him?"

"Damn right I know him. I owe that tough bastard."

"We'll keep watch over the hospital, Mr. Randisi."

"Good. Real-time monitoring of the security cameras. I want to know the where and the when."

Randisi left the computer logged on and returned to his seat. He speed dialed Ordstrom's number.

"Mr. Ordstrom, I have them located in a California hospital. We have indentified Frank Carella. And the guy we knew as Colonel Stone is there, too. Only he's registered as a Justice agent. Name of Cooper. I have them under electronic surveillance. If they leave we can track them."

"Good work, Thomas. I can tell you that Hoekken is dead. He didn't survive the Mexico mission, so it's down to you."

"I'll report in with a status update ASAP, sir."

Randisi ended the call. He pressed a button on the arm of his seat, summoning the flight steward. "Coffee. Strong. Black. You got any food?"

"I'll bring you today's menu."

Randisi was feeling good.

What the hell, he thought. Go with the flow.

24

While the chopper pilot had worked on Carella he found the man had a broken leg in addition to his shattered arm and badly gashed face. With the minimal aids in the med kit the pilot had done a satisfactory job. He had strapped up Casper's ribs and cleaned up the other wounds. Bolan had stood by, watching intently. By the time the pilot completed his care Bolan's attitude had changed toward the man. The pilot, Harry DeVoe, had worked well despite the situation.

"We need to get these two back into the U.S. To the nearest hospital."

"There's one a half-hour flight from the border crossing."

"Take us there."

With Carella and Bud Casper onboard, the helicopter had lifted off and made the trip north. DeVoe was as good at flying as he was with the med kit.

DeVoe called ahead to the hospital and advised he was coming in with injured. A team was waiting to take Carella and Bud Casper directly to the emergency department, leaving Bolan alone with the pilot.

"You've given me one hell of a problem, Harry."

DeVoe dragged off his baseball cap, scrubbing a hand through his thinning hair. He looked Bolan straight in the eyes. "Am I going to go running off and give you up?"

"Something like that."

"Why should I? The way I see it you guys have gone

through enough. And that guy, Hoekken, the one who hired me? He's the only contact I had. No other names. Just him. He paid me in cash, up-front, so I got no beef there. Okay, it was a dodgy deal, turns out. I didn't know what he was going to do after we got on your tail. When they started shooting at you…what could I do? I flew Hoekken and his crew over the border. He gave me instructions where to go and I went. I was already in the crapper by then."

"Not the first time you jumped the border?"

DeVoe grinned. "No. I did it before. Not all my charters are lily-white. Sometimes you take a chance if the money's right. It's a living and it's all I got, pal. So what you going to do, arrest me?"

"Why would you think that?"

"Because I'm starting to get the feeling you're most likely a damn cop. Or a Fed. Just a feeling is all."

"Harry, where did you see service?"

"How did you guess?"

"The way you handled the recovery. Looked after the wounded. I guess it wasn't the first time."

"Desert Storm. Yeah. Hell, somebody had to see our boys were treated right. Kids, most of 'em. I'd see them come in all bright-eyed and bushy tailed. Next time I saw them they were in the dirt with bullet holes in them. Or looking for the bits and pieces that got blown off by fuckin' mines. You know the most asked question they threw at me? *What the hell are we doing out here?* All they wanted was to go home." He stopped short, reliving unwanted memories. "That's why I helped your buddies."

"Help me some more, Harry. Fire up your bird and go home. Forget this whole trip. If your only contact was Hoekken then the less you know about this business the better. Safer for you, too. I can take it from here. Walk away and go home."

"You trust me to do that?"

The Executioner looked the pilot in the eye, then nodded.

DeVoe climbed back into the helicopter. Bolan stepped back as the rotors turned. He watched it rise and hover. DeVoe angled away, climbing quickly, the aircraft soon lost in the blue California sky.

There were times, Bolan decided, when you just had to put your trust in someone. He had experienced betrayal and mistrust over the last few days. Violence and suffering. A little faith went a long way to restore his feelings.

EVENING FOUND MACK BOLAN taking time to reflect on the day. From Puerto Laredo back to home ground, with a lot of business in between. Only now, with Casper and Frank Carella stabilized and sedated in their hospital rooms, was Bolan able to take time out for himself. The moment he relinquished the burden he felt the utter weariness wash over him. The exertions of the past hours overwhelmed his body. Bolan began to be aware of the aches from his own battered body. His own comparatively minor injuries had been tended to. Fresh clothing had been produced from the hospital's emergency supply, his own garments disposed of. The only thing he kept was his leather jacket and his weapons. He kept the pistols concealed beneath the jacket. With a mug of strong coffee he dropped into a comfortable chair in the visitors' lounge and rested.

While he sat he considered his options. Foremost in his mind was OTG. Jacob Ordstrom was not going to sit idly by and ease the pressure. He would no doubt get reports about Hoekken's failure in Mexico. He'd eventually learn that his security chief was dead. It would force Ordstrom to increase his attempt at getting to Carella and the files. No matter how he felt personally Ordstrom would never admit if he was starting to feel desperate. He always showed a hard outer persona in public. With the implications of what the files might reveal Ordstrom had too much to lose. Ordstrom was not going to go down without a fight.

A down-and-dirty fight with no concerns about collateral damage was already in evidence.

Bolan drained his coffee and put the mug aside. He reached inside his jacket, unzipping the pocket to remove the aluminum case holding the flash drives. He stared at them, nestled in the soft sponge packing.

A pair of small plastic objects were the cause of all the problems. Because of the flash drives and what they contained, people had suffered. People had died. Jacob Ordstrom had orchestrated a violent pursuit across the country. All in a desperate attempt to regain control of the files that could bring him down. His desire to control the data had resulted in the attempted wipeout of human life. He had decided the information was more important than human existence. It said a great deal about the man's disregard for others.

25

Randisi sat behind the wheel of the SUV across from the hospital. He had a laptop open and logged on beside him. The screen showed a full schematic of the hospital. It had come from Weatherby. His voice came through the headset Randisi was wearing. The direct connection with Weatherby came from a satellite uplink, making use of OTG's communications division. There was a few seconds' delay between send and receive, but the transmissions were sharp and clear.

"The outbuilding housing the backup generator is the section highlighted in red. If you disable that there won't be any power after we cut the main supply," Weatherby said.

Randisi glanced at his watch. Semidarkness shrouded the hospital building and car park, leaving only the pools of illumination from the security lights.

"Give the word and we can disable their internal and exterior cameras," Weatherby said.

Randisi acknowledged. He synchronized his watch with Weatherby.

"I'm about to drive into the parking lot. Eastern corner of the lot is at the rear of the building. Close to the generator block. As soon as I'm ready to exit the vehicle I'll give you the call. You disable the cameras. I'll take out the backup generator then you shut down the phones and the main power supply."

He started the SUV, swung it across the empty street and negotiated the entrance to the hospital parking lot. Visiting hours had ended so there were only a few vehicles parked at this hour. Randisi drove across to his chosen spot, reversing into an empty space. He cut the motor and pocketed the key.

He was dressed in a black combat suit, wool cap and rubber-soled combat boots. A snug flak vest was worn over the combat suit, courtesy, as was all his equipment, of OTG. Once he was inside the hospital building Randisi would have Stone standing between him and Carella.

There would also be the added threat of the hospital's own armed security guards. According to Weatherby there would be three of them on duty. One in the security office, with the other two on roving patrols. Once the cameras were disabled and the power cut, those guards were going to be hyped up for trouble. Randisi didn't want to be exposed to random hostile fire from the guards. The vest would help to avoid problems while he carried out his probe. A shoulder rig held a SIG Sauer P-226 complete with sound-suppressor. He had a couple of extra magazines and a keen bladed Tanto knife. A nylon bag slung from one shoulder held the tools he'd use to break in to the generator housing.

His final piece of equipment was a set of night-vision goggles. The hospital would be in near darkness but he would be able to see. It would allow him to go directly to Carella's room and deal with him. If Stone got in the way… Randisi grinned. He was counting on that happening.

Randisi opened his door and stepped out. The California night was warm, with only a faint breeze. He glanced above the hospital building. A bright moon. He might have chosen a darker aspect if he had been given the choice, but necessity demanded the operation be carried out *now*.

He moved silently behind the SUV, then stepped over the low concrete barrier that edged the parking lot. He was on the service road that ran to the back of the hospital. Pausing at the corner, Randisi opened his com set.

"Weatherby. Do it."

Weatherby acknowledged the command. There was a brief pause as the computer locked into the hospital's own system and ran its override. Then Weatherby's voice carried through to Randisi.

"Security system is down. Their cameras are blind. You're clear to move. Phone system will be down in two minutes."

Randisi moved around the corner of the building and down the service road to the brick building that housed the backup generator. At the louvered door he used the first of his tools to take out the lock. With the door free he opened it and slipped inside. The generator, housed in a steel cabinet, filled the space. Randisi went directly to the control panel set in the wall. He opened the box and disabled the controls. Behind him the standby lights on the generator winked out. Randisi took a pair of thick insulated gloves and a pair of cable shears from his bag and severed the main cable, preventing any reset of the generator.

Weatherby's measured tone came through his headset. "Phone system is down."

"Okay. I am going inside. Get the main power shut down and make sure they can't get it back on," Randisi said.

"We're on it."

Randisi edged around the building, making for the main entrance. He flattened against the outer wall, lost in the deep shadows, waiting. The hospital lights flickered briefly, then went out completely. Randisi worked the night-vision goggles into place. He let his eyes adjust to the eerie green image, his mind already calculating the short time span he would have. Once it was realized they were without lights or phones, someone would pick up a cell phone and make a call. His mission time could be counted in minutes. Randisi wanted to be in and back out without delay. He took out the sound-suppressed pistol, easing off the safety.

He moved, breaching the doors and entering the building. The image of the layout was clear in his mind. On his left the main desk. Directly ahead the wide corridor that led to all departments. His target was the patient rooms. Down the main corridor, first right. Ahead of him there was another corridor with doors on each side. He had the number of Carella's room, so that part was easy.

According to Weatherby's constant monitoring of the corridor, courtesy of the security cameras, the only visitors to Carella's room had been hospital staff and Stone. No one else. Stone himself had not left the building since arriving, so it was determined that the information Carella had with him was still within the hospital. A calculated guess, yes. It was based on the premise that Carella had kept the incriminating files with him since his dash for Mexico and his return to the U.S. The files were the reason Carella had run. His high card. He was unlikely to have relinquished his hold on those files— unless he had passed them to Stone. And from the gathered intel, Stone had only been in contact with hospital staff and had remained inside the building.

As Randisi walked by the main desk he could see the night staff milling about in confusion, their voices raised as they tried to understand what was happening. In the distance he could hear other voices. Protests. Shouts of alarm. Exactly what he needed.

Confusion.

People were unable to figure out what was happening. He moved along the main corridor, his concentration on his objective.

As a result he almost missed the uniformed security guard as the man emerged from a side passage. The man had his pistol out and there was a purpose in his stride as he cut across the corridor, directly toward Randisi. He'd noticed the dark bulk of the soldier.

"Hey, you hold on," the guard said.

Randisi brought his weapon around, saw the faint gleam of light on his hand and arm. Moonlight was ghosting through a skylight overhead. Enough to reveal Randisi's outline.

His military training clicked in. No debate. Simply a reaction. He triggered the pistol, putting a pair of 9 mm slugs into the guard. The man grunted, stumbling back against the wall. As he slid down Randisi stepped in close and put a third shot through the man's skull, then turned back on his original course. He reached the cross corridor and took the right turn. A female in hospital whites, feeling her way along the wall, loomed up in his green vision. Randisi reached out and grabbed her shoulder, spinning her to face the wall. He savagely slammed the butt of his pistol across the back of her skull. The woman shuddered, slumping to the floor.

He passed the first room, checking the number, establishing his position.

Three doors to go. He made his way down the hall. He reached out and worked the handle, felt the door swing open.

He stepped inside and scanned the room.

The bed was empty.

Son of a bitch.

He damped down on the anger that was threatening to rise. Had to stay calm. Reasoning.

Bad intel.

But Carella had to be here somewhere.

Randisi spun on his heel.

He came face-to-face with Colonel Stone.

26

Bolan had stepped out of Carella's room to get himself a cup of chilled water from the dispenser in the corridor. He was walking back to the room when he saw the red light go out on the security camera covering that section of the passage. At this time of night the main lights had already been reduced to a lower intensity. Bolan might not have noticed if the illumination had been stronger. He was also on full alert, far from being convinced that they were out of danger. He did not imagine for one second that OTG had given up. The threat from Ordstrom was still as strong as ever. So Bolan remained cautious, treating any occurrence as a possible warning.

He pulled the Beretta, working the selector to set it for single shot. He kept the weapon at his side, reluctant to advertise it to anyone who might see him. The hospital staff had enough to deal with. The last thing they needed was a show of artillery.

Bolan pushed open the door to Carella's room and looked him over. The man was still sleeping, which at this moment in time was better for him. He didn't need to know news of a possible threat. Bud Casper was in the next room. Bolan's silent inspection told him Casper was sleeping, as well.

The side corridor where patient rooms were situated ended in a blank wall. No window. The construction of the wing meant it jutted out from the main block of the building, so each of the rooms, on either side, did have windows. Bolan had checked them and found they were sealed units, with no means of entry apart from breakage.

He glanced at the security camera again, then decided to check out the next one. It was a possibility the one in his corridor was an isolated breakdown. The Executioner didn't accept such situations so easily. He reached the end of the section and checked out the next camera. No red light. It was dead, as well.

Bolan felt a stir of unease. The hospital, though small, was modern and fitted with expensive equipment. He had already learned that the place ran on a computer-controlled setup that was no more than a couple of years old.

He turned to one of the internal phones. It would do no harm to check with the front desk. The phone buzzed as he put it to his ear, his finger reaching to tap in the desk number.

Bolan pressed the button. Heard it start to ring out.

Then the phone went dead.

He worked the button again. Nothing. The phone remained silent.

His unease began to grow. One malfunction was worrying. Two were no coincidence.

Bolan found himself glancing up at the ceiling lights.

The darkness swallowed him. Seconds later he heard voices raised in alarm. Something hit the floor somewhere with a metallic sound.

The Executioner let his eyes adjust to the darkness. When he took a look around he noticed a faint glow from moonlight that was seeping in through the skylights. He stayed where he was until his vision had allowed for the illumination and retraced his steps to the door to Carella's room. The open door and the room's window let him see that Carella still slept.

Why hadn't the backup power taken over?

The emergency generator should have kicked in by now.

He knew someone had disabled it, had most likely done

that before the main power and the phones had been cut. To achieve that would have taken reach and power.

Bolan could only think of one group who could do that.

And he knew why.

OTG had traced Carella's presence in the hospital. Probably using the technology they created. Computerized tracking could have monitored the security cameras. That had infiltrated the power and telephone systems and shut them down. That would have directed their strike force to finish the job Hoekken had failed to carry out.

Jacob Ordstrom was making a last attempt at retrieving his missing data.

Bolan spun on his heels and headed along the corridor. He was heading for the opposite side of the hospital building where a similar wing held more patient rooms.

He allowed the faint moonlight penetrating the skylights to guide him, moving aside as he spotted hesitant figures coming out of the shadows. Hospital staff were trying to go about their work. The distressed calls from frightened patients filled his ears. If the power was off some of them could be in need of special care. More innocents caught up in Ordstrom's desperate bid for survival.

The second wing was in front of Bolan. He spotted a crumpled figure curled up against the wall. Bolan checked and found one of the security guards. The man was dead. Hit three times from close range. Farther on he saw another figure. Bolan crouched. A female. Dressed in hospital whites. One of the nurses. She was stirring as Bolan checked her. Blood wet on her face from a gash. Her breathing was steady.

"Stay where you are," he said. "We'll get back to you."

He straightened and headed along the corridor.

The door to the room he wanted was open.

Bolan saw a dark figure emerging from inside the room.

He saw the dull gleam of a handgun as the intruder sensed his presence.

"Glad you could make it, *Colonel Stone.*"

Bolan couldn't make out the features, but he recognized the voice.

Master Sergeant Thomas Randisi.

27

Randisi swung the sound-suppressed pistol up at Bolan. The Executioner responded by slamming the heavy Beretta down across Randisi's wrist, jarring the man's weapon from his grasp. It thudded to the floor, brushing Bolan's foot, and he kicked at it, sending the weapon sliding out of reach.

Within a heartbeat Randisi sprang forward, his left hand clamping over Bolan's wrist, forcing the barrel of the Beretta out of target range. He dug in his heels and pushed, forcing Bolan away from the door and across the darkened corridor. Bolan summoned as much resistance as he was able. His body had yet to fully recover from his Mexican experience and he was running on less than one hundred percent.

The opposite wall brought them up cold, Randisi jerking a knee up and slamming it against Bolan's hip. The blow partially numbed Bolan's leg. He reacted by hammering his left fist against Randisi's exposed jaw, the force jerking Randisi's head back. Bolan hit out again, catching Randisi on the same spot. Flesh tore at the corner of Randisi's mouth. Randisi grunted, acknowledging the pain. Before he could lower his head Bolan wedged the palm of his hand under Randisi's jaw and put everything he had into pushing the man's head up and back, putting pressure on Randisi's spine. Breath exploded from Randisi's lips. He resisted for a few seconds. Then he dropped, taking Bolan down with him. His booted feet came up, wedging against Bolan's stomach. As Randisi hit the floor, rolling back, he thrust with his feet and Bolan was thrown over him. The

Executioner gasped as the impact jarred his lungs. He landed with force enough to bounce the Beretta from his hand.

As he sucked air into his lungs Bolan heard the soft whisper of Randisi's boots as the man came after him. Bolan rolled on his side, hands bracing against the floor, and he pushed to his feet, meeting Randisi's head-on charge. They slammed together, each attempting to gain the advantage, hands seeking something to grip. Bolan spread a palm against Randisi's face, feeling the bulk of the night-vision goggles. He gripped the rubber surround and wrenched the piece of equipment from the soldier's head. At least now Randisi would be forced to work unaided in the near dark.

The move enraged Randisi. He swung a balled fist that connected with Bolan's jaw, then hammered at Bolan's ribs. The Executioner countered with a savage head-butt that split Randisi's nose. Blood sprayed from the crushed flesh. Seizing the moment, Bolan caught hold of Randisi's right arm, trapping it against the side of his body as he turned in against the man, crunching the point of his elbow into Randisi's ribs, repeating the blows until he felt bone snap. Still gripping Randisi's arm, Bolan swung him hard, slamming the man's face against the wall. Then he hammered his knee up into the base of Randisi's spine. He spread his palm against the back of Randisi's skull and rammed his face into the wall again.

Overhead the thin cloud covering the moon drifted away. Light increased and the gloom in the corridor was partly dispelled. The pale light exposed the two struggling figures. Bloody and panting as they fought.

Kicking away, Randisi forced Bolan back, then turned. Ignoring his pain, he executed a high kick that slammed into Bolan's chest. Bolan was driven backward, balance gone, and he hit the floor and slid across the smooth surface. Randisi advanced, snatching his knife from its sheath. Bolan saw the steel blade gleaming in the cold moonlight as he pushed to his feet. Behind the bloody mask Randisi's face held a wild grin as he closed in on Bolan, the knife held before him. He slashed out, feinted, then reversed his action. The blade slid across Bolan's torso, cutting though his clothing and penetrating the flesh. The cut was keenly painful. Blood surged from the wound, running hot down Bolan's flesh.

"Son of a bitch," Randisi shouted. "What did you do with that little shit? Tell me and I'll kill you fast."

"Insurance. I guessed Ordstrom wasn't about to quit so Carella went into a different room to the one listed on the computer."

Bolan used the brief verbal encounter to brace himself for Randisi's next lunge, his aching, battered body ready to react.

"You faked it. Just like you faked the CID colonel."

Randisi's anger took the sharp edge from his attack. Bolan saw it coming and dropped, the blade cutting air above his head. He rammed a hard fist into Randisi's groin, catching his genitals with a crippling blow that drew a shriek from the AWOL soldier's lips. At the same time Bolan executed a powerful leg sweep, taking Randisi's feet from under him. Randisi landed on his back, air bursting from his lungs. Remembering the deadly steel blade, Bolan hauled his body around, lunged for Randisi's knife hand, caught the wrist and locked both hands around it. He twisted the blade away from himself, dragging Randisi close, and slammed a booted foot that smacked against the side of Randisi's head. The blow was delivered with unrestrained force. Randisi grunted, his head whipping back, blood spewing from his lips as his teeth snapped down on his own tongue.

Not letting go, Bolan rammed the sole of his boot into Randisi's armpit, still wrenching at the wrist. He straightened his leg and heard the soft crunch as Randisi's arm was pulled from the shoulder socket. Randisi shuddered, his grip on the knife slackening. Bolan slammed the hand against the floor and the knife bounced free. Rolling to his knees, Bolan hauled Randisi into a sitting position, locked an arm around the man's neck and started to pull him in close. Despite having lost the use of his right arm, Randisi still had his left. It snaked up, fingers grasping the leather of Bolan's jacket. Randisi hunched his body, yanking Bolan forward and over his shoulder. Bolan was thrown, body twisting through the air. He felt himself dropping and threw his arms out in a body break to lessen the impact as he landed.

Behind him Randisi cast about for a weapon, spotting his dropped pistol. He scrambled across the floor, left arm extended as he went for the discarded sidearm.

Bolan, turning over, saw Randisi's intention and swiveled his head in the direction of his Beretta. He picked out the dark outline of the pistol yards away and, knowing his life depended on a fast reaction, he lunged for it.

Survival instinct drove both men. Neither was going to give an edge to the other. They were both trained in the killing art. Both had served in combat zones and knew the razor edge that separated the living from the dead.

This time it was the final chance.

The Executioner launched himself forward, hitting the floor in a sliding roll, fingers reaching out for the seemingly elusive Beretta.

Behind him Randisi scooped up his own gun, gripping the butt hard as he swung the muzzle in the direction of the man who had caused him nothing but grief from the moment he stepped into his life.

Randisi hauled himself upright, finger already stroking back on the trigger. He felt the pistol buck in his hand as it fired, the sound-suppressor reducing the blast noise, and knew he had missed. Randisi was a right-hand shooter. He was proficient with his left, but not quite good enough.

Bolan felt the impact of the slug as it gouged into the floor inches from his left arm. He curled his fingers around the Beretta, felt himself hit the base of the wall, arced his body around and thrust out his pistol. He pulled the trigger in the instant Randisi fired his second shot. The slug struck just over Bolan's ribs on the right side. The glancing blow gouged flesh, badly bruising the rib bones.

Randisi was ready for a third shot when he felt a solid *thump* against the flak jacket protecting him. He almost shouted his confidence at his opponent as he put pressure on the trigger.

The trigger pull didn't happen.

Randisi felt the slug core into his chest cavity. And the three further slugs that followed. Randisi stumbled back, his body reacting to the damage done by the 9 mm projectiles.

The bullets should have been stopped by the OTG body armor.

He was still wondering why they weren't as he hit the floor and started to cough up blood. As he lay there he saw the Executioner's heighted form standing over him. He couldn't move so all he did was stare up at the man who had defeated him. His body and his brain shut down.

Bolan slumped against the wall, right hand pressed over the bloody wound in his side. He was still bleeding from the knife gash, as well as from numerous tears and gouges. And he could hear a voice in his head, distant and faint, but a voice. It took him seconds to realize it was coming from where Randisi lay. Bolan leaned over and spotted the slim headset Randisi was wearing. He reached out a bloody hand and slid the headset free, working the power pack and com set from Randisi's belt. He held the headset to one ear and listened to the voice.

"Randisi, come in. We heard noise. Need a sitrep. You there?"

"Mission accomplished," Bolan said, his voice lowered to disguise it.

Bolan shut the com set down and sat waiting for someone to come and get him because at that moment he felt too damn tired to even stand up.

28

Jacob Ordstrom turned at the tapping sound on his office door. "Come in."

It was Rick Weatherby. Ordstrom tried to read the man's expression, unsure how to decipher the look in his eyes. Weatherby crossed to stand at Ordstrom's desk, fidgeting slightly.

"Well?" Ordstrom asked.

"I don't know, sir."

"Don't know what?"

"I can't give you a clear report. Everything seemed to be going well. Randisi disabled the backup generator. We cut the main power and the telephone. As soon as that was done Randisi went inside. He wasn't saying very much but I could hear background sounds through his com set. He was following our intel on the hospital layout. It would have taken him directly to Carella's room. Up to that point it was going smoothly. Then the line started to go indistinct. I heard Randisi say something that sounded like 'Glad you could make it.' After that there was too much interference. Odd sounds. I kept calling and after some time Randisi said, 'Mission accomplished.' The connection went completely dead after that."

"No contact at all?"

Weatherby shook his head.

"Not since last night. I might be wrong, sir, but the last thing Randisi said, it sounded...well, odd."

"*Odd?* Odd how?"

Weatherby rubbed his forehead. "I could have got it wrong. It had been a long shift. Randisi sounded tired. In fact I could have sworn it wasn't his voice. That was probably the poor connection we seemed to have."

"But he did say he had completed his mission?"

"Yes, sir."

Ordstrom glanced over his shoulder at a sudden sound and saw rain streaking the office window. He could see a gray sky that promised more. "Have you been monitoring the media? Anything coming through about the hospital?"

"Only vague reports from the hospital administrator about the unexpected power outage. He said it had been handled. The power was back on. No patients had been put at risk and everything was back under control."

Ordstrom smiled. "They're keeping the matter under wraps. A clampdown by the authorities. I'd guess by now the FBI will be running things. Use our connections in the Bureau. See if you can find anything out."

"Yes, sir. And Randisi?"

"Keep trying to contact him. He might be staying out of sight until he feels it safe to come in. See if he's made contact with the plane. The pilot has orders to wait until Randisi contacts him for a return flight."

Weatherby turned to leave. "Do you think we've done it, Mr. Ordstrom?"

"Cautiously optimistic, Weatherby. I won't feel entirely comfortable until I have those files back in my hands."

The door closed behind Weatherby. Ordstrom stood at the window and watched the rain hammering at the glass. It drifted across the OTG grounds in solid sheets. The gloom created by the sudden storm matched Ordstrom's own mood. He would never admit to anyone that he *was* concerned. He would be a fool not to be. Showing confidence in front of his hirelings was natural. If the commander exhibited fear, how was he expected to be able to inspire the troops? He corrected himself quickly. Fear was not the emotion he was experiencing. A little anger. Some frustration. Annoyance that this matter had gone so far before he regained control. If, as he believed, Randisi had completed his mission and the OTG data files were in his hands, then maybe there was a chance the whole damn mess could be cleared away. The incriminating evidence left in limbo in OTG's mainframe through sheer incompetence had now been completely removed. That just left Carella's damning files. If they could be deleted, too, then there would be nothing for anyone to use in order to point the finger. The peripheral damage could be handled with less fallout. If Randisi had also dealt with Carella, then that was another pawn in the game removed.

One of the phones on Ordstrom's desk rang. He picked up and recognized the measured tones of Colonel Kindred.

"David, what can I do for you?"

"You can conjure up a way we can shut down the investigation at Camp Macklin. They're turning that place inside out. And they've been asking why Francis Nelson and your man Janssen were both shot with the same rifle. One issued to our AWOL Master Sergeant Randisi. And you can tell me how to answer the questions I keep getting asked about *my* connection with OTG and you."

"How did—?"

"I don't know how. I don't know why. But someone has got the CID and Military Command all fired up. Right now the only place they haven't looked is up my ass, and I have the distinct feeling that's next. Jacob, this is serious. And it isn't going to go away. You are forever going on about the influence you have with people who matter. Start using it and call in every fucking favor you have. If you don't we are all going to be looking at the sky through steel bars."

The phone was slammed down, leaving Ordstrom staring

at his own receiver. He considered his next move. He quickly punched in a number and waited for the pickup.

"Senator Riesling's office."

"Jacob Ordstrom. Put me through to the senator, please."

"I'm sorry, Mr. Ordstrom, but the senator is not in his office at the moment. He left instructions that any calls be routed through to his personal cell phone."

"Would you connect me. It is urgent."

It took a while before a connection was made. The phone rang for an even longer time before being answered.

"Mark? Jacob, what's going on?"

"What's going on is my lawyer has told me not to talk to you. It's not in my best interests."

Ordstrom was unable to suppress a snort of laughter. "Mark, this is me. Jacob. What is this nonsense about not speaking to me?"

"There have been accusations laid at my door that I may be indicted by a grand jury over my involvement with you. The words 'against the national interest' have been raised. Do you understand what that means?"

Ordstrom was silent for a moment, allowing the words to sink in.

"Goodbye, Jacob. Do *not* call me again," the senator said.

Ordstrom sat down. The son of a bitch. He recalled Kindred's terse comments.

The bastards were always there when it came to payout time. With a hint of trouble in the air the two of them had walked away, leaving Ordstrom to pick up the pieces.

He stood again and crossed to the wet bar on the other side of his office. He chose an expensive malt whiskey, a large tumbler, and returned to his desk. He poured himself a large measure, took a generous swallow and began to work through his options.

How damn fast things could fall apart, he thought.

His ordered and well-controlled life was being pulled apart. Little by little. With each passing minute a layer was being stripped away. The so-called loyalty of his business partners had already eroded. Riesling and Kindred were the first. He thought of others who had benefited from their association with OTG. Men who had profited well. He wondered how soon it might be before his phone started ringing again as they all cried off. If official investigations continued at the pace that had drawn in Riesling and Kindred it would be soon.

"Jacob, you will be the lone voice crying in the wilderness of betrayal," he said out loud, realizing he had emptied his whiskey tumbler. "Have another. Thanks, I will."

Behind him the afternoon became darker. Ordstrom swiveled his chair around to view the spread of the plant. Rain, the heaviest fall he had seen for some time, obscured his vision. Dark, swollen clouds filled the sky. He held the bottle in his hand, refilling his tumbler, savoring the rich scent of the whiskey as it spilled out.

"Are we quitting?" Ordstrom laughed at the question. *"Hell, no."*

When the phone rang Ordstrom was jolted out of his reflective mood. He turned his chair around and picked up.

"Randisi won't be reporting in," the voice said. "I'm standing in for him."

"Who the fuck are you?" Even as he formed the question it all fell into place.

He knew who was on the phone.

He also knew that Frank Carella was still alive and the missing data files were in official hands.

When his office door opened to admit the tall, dark-haired figure Ordstrom realized he was looking at the man who had taken down both Hoekken and Randisi. He surprised himself by topping up his tumbler and raising it in a greeting.

"Do I call you Stone or Cooper?"

"Makes no difference," Bolan said.

Ordstrom studied the man. The Executioner's face showed the results of his final clash with Randisi. It was bruised and raw. What Ordstrom didn't see was the dressing that covered the bullet wound in his side, or the stitches that had closed the knife wound. What he did see was the hard gleam in the big man's blue eyes. Eyes that showed no pity.

Bolan raised his left hand from where it had hung partially covered behind his back. It held a bulky object. Bolan tossed it onto Ordstrom's desk. It landed with a thud, scattering items from the polished surface, knocking over the bottle of whiskey. Amber liquid pooled across the desk.

"Recognize it?" Bolan asked.

"Should I?"

Ordstrom knew what the object was even before he spread it across the desk. A flak jacket. By the logo inside it was an OTG product.

"What am I supposed to do? Wear it?"

"Not recommended. Randisi had it on when we met up at the hospital."

Ordstrom's gaze was drawn to the ragged holes in the jacket. A faint shiver of apprehension chilled him as he turned over the flaps and saw that the holes went all the way through.

"You mistakenly supplied your man with one of your own substandard jackets. The kind you've been issuing under OTG contracts to American soldiers. Nice touch, Ordstrom."

Ordstrom's hand moved across the surface of the jacket, fingers touching the ragged holes.

"I can't deny the evidence when it's right in front of me." He raised his eyes to Bolan. "But I hope you have more than just this," he said out of sheer bravado.

"Since yesterday the files Frank Carella kept with him while your kill teams chased him are being checked out by people who have no association with you, or OTG. Kindred and Riesling are surrounded by their lawyers and names are starting to fall out of the trees."

"Cooper, you'll never understand why I acted the way I did."

"Make your excuses to Francis Nelson. To Veronica Carella. Cal Ryan. You ordered their deaths. Make your excuses to all the other people hurt since this started."

"Am I supposed to experience a startling revelation about the evil of man? Don't expect it, Cooper. I didn't get where I am by worrying about collateral damage. People die every day. For all sorts of reasons. They starve to death. Are wiped out by disease. Do we worry about them?" Ordstrom waved an arm at the office window. "You understand what's out there? It's more than a factory. It's a complex empire I created from nothing. It has to be maintained. I work with the military. The government. I broker deals with other countries. This Carella affair has been a damned irritation. I'll grant you those files will cause a great deal of harm. Embarrassment, too, if names start coming up. But Carella and the others don't matter. They're unimportant. What's that phrase? They're just 'the little people,' Cooper. OTG is too big to be put at risk by their kind. Too important to a lot of powerful people. That's why it has to be kept alive, and I'm doing it. Cooper, you have to realize I'm so well-covered here I'll walk away somehow."

"I was afraid you might say that."

The door swung open and Rick Weatherby rushed into the office. He held a pistol in his right hand.

"He's on site, sir. Cooper. Used some kind of Justice Department credentials to—"

Bolan turned to meet the man's full-on rush. Weatherby was raising the weapon when Bolan drove his right fist into his face. The thud of the blow was heavy. Weatherby stumbled back, blood starting to gush from his mashed nose and torn lips, eyes already glazing over. He offered no resistance when

Bolan moved in close and delivered a couple more solid blows that put the man on the floor.

Jacob Ordstrom lunged for the pistol. He aimed at Bolan and ranted about OTG's power and his own importance.

Bolan grabbed his Beretta 93-R. "I don't need an excuse. Your guilt has already been established. I'm here to see you accept your judgment," he told Ordstrom.

The Beretta delivered a single 9 mm slug. It cored in through Ordstrom's forehead before he could pull the trigger. He fell back across his executive chair, eyes still wide open and staring.

He didn't see Mack Bolan turn away and leave the office, closing the door behind him as he walked away.

Epilogue

"They won't go down without a fight," Dane Nelson said. He stood alongside Hal Brognola at his son's grave, in full uniform. His shoulder was still heavily bandaged, his arm held immobile. "With Ordstrom dead and data in the public arena, the people behind him will find it hard to stay in the shadows."

"Cal Ryan's evidence will help, as well," the big Fed said. "He wrote up what Francis passed along and sent an encrypted file to his editor. That's been released now."

"They'll close ranks. Use all the influence they can to stay out of the spotlight. Hal, you understand the way the military works if it comes under scrutiny. Even I'm getting the cold shoulder. People I've known for years walk away when they see me coming. They're all scared of getting dragged into the whole sorry mess. Since Kindred started to talk there's been a shutdown on information being allowed out."

"Full details have been passed to the White House. The president has been fully briefed. Deniability is not going to work the whole way down the line. Carella is still willing to give his evidence to back those files. He'll have to do it from his hospital bed."

"How is he?"

"He took some punishment but he's one tough guy. Better since his girlfriend showed up."

"Your other friend?"

"He's fine. Bud Casper's going to be laid up for a couple of weeks, though. His main concern is getting his plane back out of Mexico. He doesn't know it yet but that's already happening."

"Hal, I put in for retirement. And don't say a word. I can't offer anything more to the army. Sitting behind that desk has already started to harden my arteries. With Francis gone there isn't much to look forward to. So I'll collect my pension and go up to the lake house. Leave the in-fighting to those who want it."

"Sounds like a good idea, Dane. I might even come and visit," Hal said.

"*Might?* Hal, you *will* visit. That's my last official order. Next time we meet I'll be plain *Mr.* Dane Nelson."

They stood and paid their respects to Francis Nelson in silence.

TAKE 'EM FREE

2 action-packed novels plus a mystery bonus

NO RISK

NO OBLIGATION TO BUY

AleX Archer
SACRED GROUND

The frozen north preserves a terrible curse…

For the Araktak Inuits, the harsh subzero tundra is their heritage. Now a mining company has purchased the land, which includes the sacred Araktak burial site. Contracted by the mining company, archaeologist Annja Creed is to oversee the relocation of the burial site—but the sacred ground harbors a terrible secret….

Available March 2010 wherever books are sold.

GOLD EAGLE®

www.readgoldeagle.blogspot.com

GRA23